ABHORRENT SIREN

JOHN BALTISBER(

St. Rooster Books

Published by St. Rooster Books.
ISBN: 978-1-955745-02-4

Copyright © 2021 John Baltisberger
Cover by Rooster Republic Press
Edited by Lisa Lee Tone

First Edition
Contact St. Rooster Book at Tim-Murr @ live . com

Dedicated to Edward Lee,

Who taught me that the only limit to writing a story was the limits I put on myself.

Chapter 1

Barbara laid her head against the wall of the bathroom stall and bit back the urge to scream; every day here was her hardest day. When she had first signed the papers to go to nursing school, she had imagined herself like a kind of graceful angel, sweeping into rooms to save lives, covering doctors' asses, and being loved by everyone. When she finally started working, she spent the first three months crying herself to sleep every night. It wasn't the hours. She could handle that. She could even handle how brusque and rude many of the doctors were. She had grown up a petite blond in the South, she was used to men viewing her as a thing to acquire and serve them. She had not been prepared for the sheer malice of the patients. Or the politics of the nurses. She came to work because she wanted to do good, but she felt beaten down every minute of every day. That was before the politics of the hospital had forced her out and she went to work for the methadone clinic. Here it was worse.

Here the patients actively hated her for trying to help them. She wasn't curing anyone or saving lives, she was just transferring one addiction into another and trying to keep from getting any patient's bodily fluids on her. At least the doctors here weren't trying to sleep with her, but the patients could sometimes be aggressive. Over the course of her three years here at the clinic, she had become as good of friends with Bruno, the security guard, as possible. He was a little full of himself, but he was also kind, and old enough to be her father, which he at least seemed to keep in mind. Barbara didn't know how much protection he would actually be, but she felt a little safer with him watching her back.

Barbara felt like she had thrown away her twenties. Swiftly approaching thirty with no social life outside of her loser boyfriend, Owen, no career prospects, and a deep and abiding hatred for her job, her biggest struggle now was with depression. Reaching into her pocket, she thumbed the little prescription bottle filled with antidepressants. She didn't want to take them. She felt like she would be admitting her mistakes if she did, she would be throwing in the towel. She carefully wiped away her tears and reapplied her makeup in a small hand mirror. She had become an expert in that; she would be damned if anyone would see her cracks.

"Hey, Barb," Bruno called as she stepped back into the hall.

"What's up?" she asked, looking up at the large man.

"We had to kick out Mr. Northrup, he was getting violent, and Ms. Sloan is getting a little restless because we're so backed up today. Do you think you could work her in a little earlier?" Bruno didn't have to play nurse's assistant, and Barbara knew several of the other nurses and doctors found his attempts at working above his job to be a nuisance, they had charts and a reason for everything they did. But Barbara drank in the kindness wherever she could get it.

"I'll check in with her. Thanks, Bruno. I—" She was interrupted by the figure of Carl Northrup kicking open the front door of the clinic, bright red blood splashed across the front of his shirt and face. Bruno turned in surprise and put a hand on his taser reflexively. Withdrawal didn't usually go this violently, unless he had snuck out to a drug dealer and taken something else which was driving him.

There was silent moment before Carl raised his hand, a hand that seemed massive and malformed, like more fingers were trying to burst out of the skin. The entire arm bulged with bizarre musculature and throbbed with veins that had long since begun to collapse from his heroin addiction. The silence was broken as Carl turned and swiped at a fellow patient and their head splattered against the wall with a sickening crunch. Bits of brain matter and shards of broken skull slowly slid down the wall as all hell broke loose.

Screams filled the air as Barbara fell on her ass and tried to pull herself away from the scene of carnage that was unfolding. Carl let loose a scream himself, though it seemed impossible for a human mouth to emit the trilling multi-tonal scream that vibrated her skull behind the eyes. Carl was moving to the next nearest person when Bruno let loose with the taser. It didn't seem to have any effect at all, other than to get Carl's attention, but if he were on PCP, it wouldn't even slow him down. He turned his eyes—pinpricks of bloodshot violence— towards Bruno and released another of his inhuman screams before dashing forward and slamming into the older, bigger man. Blood sprayed against Barbara as the wildly malformed hand of the addict pushed all the way through Bruno's chest. Blood, broken pieces of ribs, and viscera fell to the ground, and Carl let out an ear-shattering howl of triumph and turned towards another patient.

Barbara scrambled to crawl under the front desk and huddled there, covering her ears and closing her eyes against the maddening assault happening on just the other side of the desk. Even with her ears plugged, she could hear the screams from Carl and the other patients who were unable to hide like she was. Several had made a run for the door, and she prayed they would be able to escape what was happening. Then there was silence, or near silence. As she lowered her hands and opened her eyes, she could see mangled remains of a doctor that had been thrown over the desk to land near her. He was twisted and mangled so badly that she only knew who he was by the white lab coat and blood-smeared name tag. The only thing she could hear was the sound of panting. She was sure it was Carl. He had killed everyone else in the waiting room, he would find her soon, and when he did, she would die just like Bruno, messily and alone. Her entire life would amount only to what little she had accomplished so far: nothing.

After what felt like an eternity, the panting began to recede. She heard the doors of the clinic open, and then the only sound she could hear was full-throated sobs coming from somewhere in the waiting room. It took her several moments to realize they belonged to her.

**

Laura sat on the toilet, staring straight ahead. He had stopped knocking on the door and calling for her about thirty minutes ago, but she was still angry. No, she was still furious. He had accused her of being an addict, but she wasn't doing anything illegal. She wasn't shooting up or snorting anything. She was taking medicine. The doctor had *given* it to her. Of course, her knee was healed, but she still had pain. Really, she had even more pain now, her whole body ached, and times like now, the emotional pain felt like too much. There was a cold hand made of pistons and gears squeezing the life out of her heart, while her lungs refused to expand, robbing her of any breath. She was tired of his accusations. She was tired of the snide glances he shot her. He thought he was better than her? She wasn't the one who still smoked pot with her high school friends like some washed up adolescent. If anyone was a drug addict, it was him. He was supposed to be her husband, not this distant judge who made her feel like shit. But she didn't have to put up with it. She could take the *medicine* that the *doctor* had prescribed her and she wouldn't fucking care. The pain, all the pain would just go away. She wiped at her eyes with the back of her hand, smearing salty tears and trails of mascara across her face.

When she looked at her face and saw the mussed makeup, eyes red from crying, and the way her cheeks had begun to hollow, she pushed it aside. That pain would go away too. She didn't need to care, and if he didn't like it, that was his problem. He was supposed to be her safe place, her anchor. Her need for the Vicodin was as much his fault as anything else. If he didn't like it, he should be better.

***

Ferdinand 'El Guapo' Sila stood on the edge of the river watching the current carrying its debris towards the Gulf for several minutes. 'El Guapo' was not a terribly kind nickname. He was athletically built and might be considered a good looking man if not for the ragged scar that ran from the side of his jaw all the way to his hairline. A reminder of what happened when you pissed off the local drug dealers that greeted him every time he saw his reflection. Still, here on the border of Texas and Mexico, he had gotten off lightly. There were plenty of men who had lost their lives or families to the cartels or to the scum that called themselves militias. He watched the waters of the Rio Grande moving and wondered how many were buried under these waters. Hopefuls who didn't make it across the water, either gunned down or dumped here. A mass grave given anonymity by its very nature. These waters, nearing 60 feet deep in places, were murky along this stretch. The mud kicked up from the currents and disturbed by his team's equipment made it impossible to see more than a few feet down into the water.

Several months ago, fish that didn't look right had been fished out of the Gulf, a normally fresh water animal pulled out of the salty gulf waters, healthy but aggressive. All the testing done on the animal had pointed towards contaminates here in the river.

The fish that had been dissected had huge amounts of narcotics and opioids in their systems. Despite the memes about PCPisces and Meth-ladon fish, it was a serious problem. The cartels had always used the rivers to transport drugs and other illicit materials, throwing drugs and contraband overboard when authorities neared. The United States Fish and Wildlife Service had called in some of the best marine biologists and aquatic environmental scientists they could get their hands on to look into the cause of these mutations. Ferdinand and his team had been traveling down the Rio Grande River for two weeks; so far it had been a fairly fruitless search. The fish in this area seemed normal; though they were finding more than trace amounts of opioids in the fish, there was no sign of the serious mutation or adaptations they were seeing in the gulf.

Ferdinand always worried about this sort of thing: evolution's hand being forced by artificial means. When he had first heard of eugenics, it had blown his mind that so many species mankind had domesticated over the millennia were nothing like those that had existed early in our relationship with the species. Selective breeding and cross pollination to create bigger and sweeter fruits. Hormones and chemicals to ensure our beef livestock was massive and just the right flavor. The very concept was what drove him originally towards biological studies. Then, upon realizing the oceans were likely the final frontier of zoological study, he had focused into marine biology. He had hoped to be the next superstar of science, discovering new species, pressing forward the bounds of scientific understanding and exploration.

Ten years into his career, he now understood that

the only people who became superstars were the people working on pop-tech. People like Steve Jobs or Elon Musk. He had published papers, made startling discoveries that had changed the way the scientist worked with animals in brackish environments. He had been part of teams that had delved deeper into the depths of the ocean than any other scientist before him. But at the end of the day, the only people who knew his name were other marine biologists and the people working under him.

"El Guapo! Hey, El Guapo! Come here quick." Running up the bank towards him was a member of the hardware team, the group of men who were handling all of their equipment—roadies for scientists.

"Sila," he corrected gently. He hated the mockery of the nickname. It was one thing for people to call him that behind his back, but to his face, it was just an insult that he didn't have to take.

"Doctor Sila ..." The man was panting. "Come quick, the team has dredged some fucked up stuff up."

Ferdinand's face remained carefully blank, warring between exasperation that he had to work with people with such disregard for the scientific process and excitement that maybe now there would actually be something worth studying.

He hurried up the bank of the Rio Grande, abandoning his nihilistic thoughts to the currents of the river to rejoin his team. As he approached, he saw the entire team huddled around one of the specimen tanks they had set up outside their mobile lab RV.

"Okay, we found something?" Ferdinand asked as he approached.

"Doctor Sila, yes, oh my god!" Morgan, one of the junior scientists, answered.

"Yeah, holy shit." That was from an intern, Jordan.

Ferdinand rolled his eyes as he tried to push his way through the crowd of chattering scientists. Before he could, his elbow was grabbed and pulled away.

"Ferdinand, this is it."

He looked down into the excited face of his partner in this work and one of his oldest friends, Lisa Chibuzo. She was a brilliant scientist and technically his boss on this project; her knowledge and expertise lay in rivers and freshwater biology, whereas he had headed out into the great salty expanses of the world. If not for her, he probably wouldn't be here at all. He would be out in the gulf looking for more specimens if he was involved at all.

"You found adapted fish?" he asked as he continued to crane his neck to see into the tank.

"Siren, lesser siren, native to this area, but well ..." her accent, colored by learning English second hand in the schools of South Africa, was light and lilting but trembling with an infectious excitement.

He couldn't wait any longer and pushed his way to the tank. Siren are amphibians related to salamanders and not at all uncommon in the water ways of Texas. But as he got close to the tank, he was immediately taken aback. The thing in the tank was definitely a siren: resembling an eel with short, powerful front legs, no hind legs, and frond-like frills just behind its bullet shaped head. That was where normalcy ended.

The siren in the tank was dozens of times bigger than an ordinary siren. Ferdinand glanced at the scale reading and saw that the creature weighed thirty pounds and was at least five feet long. The largest lesser siren that had been caught couldn't be much longer than two feet. This thing was tremendous. And glowing. It lay curled in the bottom of the tank, and despite its dark dusty skin, Ferdinand could easily see its circulatory system, which seemed to glow with some internal red light, causing the creature to pulse with every heartbeat. Ferdinand stared for several minutes as the interns and other team members chattered about this find. This was unlike anything anyone had ever seen before. This could be the discovery that mattered.

He paused, noticing something else strange.

"Are those scales?" he asked, trying to get a clearer look in the tank. Siren were amphibians, not fish or reptiles, and their skin was usually smooth like an eel.

"Yes, El Guapo," Jordan responded, too taken by the creature in the tank to realize he had used Ferdinand's hated nickname.

Lisa stepped in to answer before Ferdinand could reprimand Jordan. "We haven't had a chance to do a dissection yet, but they appear to be translucent scales, almost an armor plating. Which would make this a completely new species of siren."

"Or something that looks like a siren. Just one?" Ferdinand asked.

"No, there were four of them, and I think we'll find more," Morgan answered. "I have a team going through the collection nets now."

He nodded at her answer and grabbed the handle of the cart the tank rested on. "I think you should all get back to work. Doctor Chibuzo and I will study this specimen." He exchanged a meaningful glance with Lisa before wheeling the tank into their mobile lab. They would do a first dissection here, but they would likely need to take all of these specimens to the NOAA laboratory in Galveston to really do a deep dive into what was going on with this discovery. But in the meantime, they could get some sort of start.

***

Mike sat on the couch. He felt hollow himself. The woman he loved was disappearing. When she was at work, she was a dynamo who only cared about success; and then she came home, popped her pills, and faded to not caring about anyone or anything. On his knee, his 6-year-old daughter bounced, her full attention on the Gameboy in her hands, volume turned up as loud as it would go. He would normally wrestle with her to get the volume to a reasonable level while he watched the news. But he was spent. He didn't have the energy to argue or fight anymore. He reached down and wrapped her head in the crook of his elbow to give her a kiss on the top of her head. The news anchor was talking about how a young woman had suffered from seizures before being rushed to the hospital due to an allergy to

14

opioids. Her local water supply had been tainted. He turned off the TV. Mike was trying to distract himself from what was happening in his home, not dwell on it.

He heard the bathroom door open. She would either come out sober and swinging, ready to continue the fight even with Abby there, or she would be high and would sink into her recliner and stare at the TV, on or off, for the rest of the evening. He loved her, but what was there to love? Every minute with her was either conflict or nothing. There was no intimacy left, there was no kindness. He watched Laura come out from the restroom; she didn't make eye contact, her jaw was relaxed. High it was.

"Hi, Mommy!" Abby called, not looking up from her game.

"Hi, baby."

"What's are we having for lunch?"

"Dinner, honey, dinner is the next meal," Mike corrected gently, hiding his heartbreak by parenting.

"Ask your dad, he's making dinner. I'm not hungry," Laura responded as she curled into her chair and pulled the fleece blanket around herself with a sigh of contentment.

Mike didn't mind cooking. Laura's job had always been more demanding and had placed him in the house with time to make dinner while she was still working.

"How about hot dogs?" he asked Abby, his eyes on the woman who was his wife. Not a great dinner, but he was too tired to dick around with cooking; he was emotionally exhausted from trying to explain to Laura that her habit was no longer medicinal, it was a leech on their family's life, killing any vestige of the relationship they once shared.

"Yaaaaay, hot dogs!" Abby responded before leaning against him.

Mike smiled at her, attempting to swallow the lead in his throat so he could function. He would love to escape this place, get away from Laura and her empty-eyed looks of apathy. But he couldn't leave Abby, he couldn't trust Laura to care for her anymore, and besides that, he still had hope she would realize what was happening and get help. He stayed for his daughter and for the memory of the woman he had married. He relocated Abby to the couch and rose to go to the kitchen. Space was always good. Maybe with enough space, Laura would realize what she was losing. He doubted she was capable of caring anymore. About him, about Abby, about anything.

***

Standing over the table, Lisa watched Ferdinand work. He was a steady hand. He had seen some spectacularly weird things in his time out at sea, but in her opinion, he had missed his calling as a surgeon. Lisa moved around the table, watching Ferdinand scrape the scales on the stomach with the fine edge of the scalpel, to no effect. He spoke calmly for the audio recorder's sake, but his voice trembled with excitement.

"The scales on the belly appear to be finer and

thinner than those on the upper part of the body and have the same translucent quality as those elsewhere."

When they had come in, Ferdinand had set up the dissection station and equipment while Lisa recorded all relevant data and observations of the living creature. Once they were both done with set up, Ferdinand drained the tank, sealed it, and pumped in carbon monoxide to peacefully and painlessly put the siren to sleep. As soon as the creature expired, the glow of its circulatory dimmed and finally disappeared. Ferdinand, who had studied deep sea creatures, was familiar with bioluminescence; it generally wasn't connected to the circulatory system, but in current circumstance, the simplest explanation was that there was some organ attached to the circulatory system that was producing luciferin within the blood, so when the heart stopped, the chemical stopped being produced, leading to the dying of the light.

Now with its legs and tail pinned on the table, the two scientists considered how they were going to manage a dissection when the thing's scales deflected their scalpels.

Lisa orated for Ferdinand as he fetched the tools needed to dissect an armor-plated animal. "The scales are hard enough to stop a reasonable amount of pressure with a scalpel. I would surmise this adaption is akin to armor plating, giving the siren an extra layer of protection. As such, we will need to de-scale the animal before proceeding. We will use some caution as it is possible this species has the tetrodotoxin found in some salamander species."

Carefully, Ferdinand scraped the scales of the underside of the creature away until the ragged and torn flesh of the belly lay exposed and ready for the knife. He offered Lisa an easy smile, as if to say 'No worries, just a new adaption.' Now they could get to the literal and figurative meat of the matter. Slicing open the belly, he looked over the insides of the siren. Things seemed to mostly make sense at first glance, except ...

He reached over and grabbed a pair of tweezers to grip a small tendril of what looked like algae that was clinging to the intestines.

"What the hell?" he asked under his breath before clearing his throat and speaking into the recorder. "Subject exhibits thin membrane growths along organs that resemble algae on first inspection. Purpose of growth is currently unknown." He used the scalpel to sever the connection and place the membrane on a petri dish, then passed it to Lisa.

As Ferdinand continued to work on the dissection, Lisa began to study the pieces of the specimen he was passing her, typing with one hand on her tablet. It was incredible and unlike any lesser siren she had observed before. While there were fish that could live in fresh and salt water, she had never seen an amphibian that was adapted to both. Not quite as sturdy as a tardigrade, but this thing could live in pretty much any moist environment.

The membrane wrapped around the organs of the siren seemed even more prevalent in the circulatory system. At first, she thought it might be some form of filter, something that leeched pollutants out of the system,

Then they got to the lungs.

"Incredible. Where the lungs should be, there are two masses of the same material as the membrane that has been described earlier, roughly five to six centimeters by three centimeters. The masses are sponges, and I don't see any signs of traditional lungs within the specimen ... Dr. Chibuzo?"

Lisa came around the table to peer down into the insides of the siren and nodded her agreement, speechless in her astonishment for a few moments. Then, she rushed back to a centrifuge she had set up to look at the results coming up on her laptop.

"The membrane is structurally similar to algae, though definitely part of the animal, but it appears to contain a high amount of carbon, luciferins, and ..." Lisa paused and looked at the readout once again. "Freddy, this animal is producing lachryma papaveris." She glanced at Ferdinand, who was looking at her blankly. She was one of the few people he allowed to use his hated childhood nickname, but it was clear he was racking his brain for where he had heard that term before. "Opium, this siren is producing opium."

Ferdinand put his scalpel down and sat on a nearby stool, staring at the table. What they were talking about was no simple adaption but a full-fledged evolution of a species into something completely new. They couldn't call this animal part of the siren family; it had scales and a completely new form of respiration never seen before. If what Lisa had discovered and was suggesting was true, it meant this creature was as much a plant as it was an amphibian. And if the presence of raw opium in the animal did point towards it being produced by the animal itself ...

"Let's get as many specimens as we can transport and get back to Galveston. We'll need a batrachologist, maybe a mycologist, and at least one geneticist," Lisa said, coming to the same conclusions Ferdinand had come to.

Ferdinand nodded and began packing things up as Lisa fired off several emails. Within the next couple of hours, they would be on their way east, back towards civilization.

***

Mike sat at the dinner table with Abby, in silence. Well, he was silent. Abby was never silent; it didn't seem she had the capability to be silent. Every minute of every day she filled the air with talk about whatever weird stories she was making up about whatever game she had downloaded on one of their phones. Sometimes it got to be too much, sometimes he just needed a second to think without that second being filled with stories about a werewolf princess pony. Which is what she was talking about now. Werewolf princess ponies and the various rules of feeding them—they didn't like hot dogs, you see. He nodded and offered the occasional affirmative to indicate he was paying attention and in fact did care very much about the care and feeding of werewolf princess ponies. He sighed and rose, grabbing a plate he had made; he didn't know why he bothered.

From the living room, a dull red glow lit everything. Mike assumed Laura had fallen asleep watching some sort of documentary on serial killers, which is what she usually did. Once upon a time, she had watched shows like *Intervention*, but those were probably a bit too close to home now.

"I made you a plate," he called, not expecting an answer.

"Hungry." Laura's voice sounded pained, like it was agony to talk.

"What?" Mike asked, feeling like a jackass as soon as he said it.

He moved toward the living room to check on Laura but didn't make it to the door. Something fast and strong slammed into his chest, flinging him across the dining room and into the wall, knocking the wind and sense out of him. Abby started screaming.

"HUNGRY!" Laura screamed at him from the doorway. But it wasn't Laura, not really. Her body was twisted, her limbs had too many elbows and joints; it reminded him of something out of a documentary about the world's scariest spiders. And she glowed, a steady pulse of angry red that leaked from her mouth and eyes and from under her skin.

Mike scrambled to his feet, ignoring the pain in his chest, the way agony stretched up from his ribs and into his brain, screaming at him that he needed to stay still. His body didn't see what he saw. Laura was crawling over the table towards Abby, a jumble of angled joints and clacking fingers, her face twisted into a bony-

21

mandibled thing. He leapt over the table and crashed into Laura, knocking her off the table and onto the floor while his own body slid across the wooden tabletop.

"Run, Abby!" he cried, and was so grateful that she didn't argue. She just got up and ran.

Mike was about to scramble to his feet to follow when he felt Laura's fingers wrap around his ankle. He gritted his teeth and instead reached for the nearest thing he could use in self defense, a fork. Thank god Abby liked to eat her hot dogs with a fork. He turned in Laura's grip as she pulled him closer, her teeth and mandibles clicking with excitement as drool pooled under her gaping maw. Mike kept his arms up, protecting his head from the blows that her deceptively strong and scrawny limbs rained down on him. At the last moment, as he saw her head dipping to bite into him, he jabbed forward, stabbing at her eyes with the fork.

Laura let out an inhuman shriek, scrambling back away from Mike, the fork still jutting from her eye socket. The blood that flowed from it pulsed, seeming to glow with an inhuman hate. Mike stood shakily, moving around the table to keep some distance between them. What had happened to his wife?

"Hunger ..." Laura murmured, but even that was difficult to make out with her mouth's new configuration. She was rising from the ground, growling and taking a step towards Mike. Mike didn't wait for her to get up. He ran and pushed through the swinging kitchen door on his way out. He needed to get to the bedroom. He could hear her behind him, the clack of newly sprouted talons on linoleum as she followed him into the kitchen. Laura slipped and slid on the tile—it would have been funny if she wasn't a grotesque inhuman monster hungry for the flesh of his daughter.

Mike didn't look back, he just ran through the house to his bedroom, Laura hot on his heels. He stopped in front of the big dresser Laura had inherited from her mother and reached up, his hands searching the unseen top of the dresser. Every second, she was getting closer. Mike shut his eyes, praying, hoping, and then his fingers closed around what he was looking for.

It was too late.

Something punched into his side, puncturing him and dragging him back from the dresser. Mike bit back a scream of terror and pain as he was spun to face the thing that was once his wife. The fork was still lodged in her skull, but new eyes had grown. They bulged with misshapen irises and blinked asynchronously. He could feel the blood streaming freely from his side where some limb had skewered him. He felt weak, his body traveling towards shock. But not while Abby was in danger.

"I'm sorry, Laura ... I love you." He lifted the gun he had grabbed from the top of the dresser, angling it under what was left of her chin, and emptied the entire magazine into her head. Bone, brain, and blood sprayed the ceiling and rained down on them.

Mike staggered back away from the mutated and mutilated thing his wife had become, clutching his side.

He wasn't done. He had to check on Abby, had to make sure she was safe. He moved through the house, dialing 9-1-1 on his cell phone as he looked for his daughter.

John Baltisberger

Abhorrent Siren

Chapter 2

Barbara watched the emergency crews work
from the back of an ambulance. The rescue crews
were swarming over the building, carting dead body
after dead body out of her clinic. Friends, patients,
coworkers. Carl Northrop had destroyed so many
lives in a few short minutes. And why? What had
happened to his arm to send him into such a frenzy?
While Northrop had always been an asshole, someone
who was rude, short, and always felt entitled, he had
never been violent or dangerous before today. His arm
had looked deformed, but maybe it had just been the
sudden violence of the moment. Maybe it had been
fear. The police had arrived first, and then most of
them had left when reports came in of another attack,
probably Carl savaging another place, killing more
people. It wasn't like Barbara hadn't seen PCP users
before, she just had never seen so much violence done
so quickly by one man.

She was wrapped in a blanket. The EMTs had been
surprised that the lone survivor of Carl's rampage
had been a petite brunette in scrubs but had acted

swiftly to get her checked out. Once they realized none of the blood on her was hers, they had wrapped her in a blanket and ignored her. They were checking everybody for signs of life, even though it was painfully obvious that none would exhibit any. They were in too many pieces. She stared off into the middle distance, the sounds of the early San Antonio morning washing over her in waves, sometimes drowning out the sounds of the bustle around her.

"Ma'am?"

Barbara snapped back to the present. There was a woman in a smart suit, her hair and makeup perfect, and behind her stood a burly man holding a camera. The news crews had arrived like vultures.

"Hi, I'm Kristina LaVaca with Channel Four Morning news; we're just going to ask you a few questions." The woman smiled in a completely insincere way.

Her perfect teeth made Barbara angry. Why didn't she go that route? She could have been self serving, gone into a career that wouldn't have her attacked by junkies. She just stared at the reporter.

"I don't think I'm up to answer any questions, actually," she finally said, when she could find her voice, when it was clear they wouldn't leave on their own.

"Oh, we just want to understand what happened here, that's all, nothing personal." Barbara must have made a face, because the kindness left Kristina's eyes. She looked like she was about to respond, demand that Barbara answer her questions, when an inhuman scream sounded through the air.

Barbara shrank back, recognizing the echoing cry. She reached out and slammed the doors of the ambulance closed, watching through the tinted glass.

Across the parking lot, three figures staggered towards the crowd of emergency responders and news crews. The three, two men and one woman, convulsed as though their muscles fought them with each step, muscles that contorted and bulged unnaturally. Just under the skin, their veins seemed to throb with an unnatural red light that gave them an infernal glowing appearance. Mouths hung open in a desperate attempt to get enough oxygen in, but also revealed a double row of horrid teeth jutting out of the gums at odd angles. The front row seemed mostly human, yellowed and broken from the lack of care common in addicts, while the back row appeared for all the world like a random collection of canines and jagged bone. Every inhale was a scrape and ragged gasp, every exhale a keening discordant scream that echoed across the parking lot.

The police who had stayed behind began shouting for the three to stop, pointing their guns, and when that was ineffective, they opened fire. But as soon as the first gun went off, the three inhuman monsters reacted, no longer shuffling but loping towards the crowds.

In a second, they were among them.

Hands that had too many fingers tipped in

28

unnatural growths swiped through an EMT who
moved too slow to dodge, cutting her in half in one
motion and flinging her torso across the lot with
trailing intestines the only link to her pelvis and legs.
The creature leapt from that kill onto a policeman, tore
into his throat with a mouth that seemed to stretch
too wide, and put that second row of teeth to work
ripping and tearing away the flesh.

The police, now panicked, were firing at the
things as quickly as they could. Blasting into the
crowd. Doing as much damage to civilians and first
responders as the creatures themselves. The bullets
tore chunks out of the things, and gobbets of flesh
flecked with glowing blood splattered the civilians
who fled in every direction. Barbara watched as
Kristina LaVaca and her cameraman tried to catch it
all on video, but whatever Kristina was saying was
hardly audible over the muffled screams and gunshots
that made it through the doors of the ambulance. Why
weren't they running? Didn't they understand these
things would kill everyone here?

Barbara couldn't see much over the shoulder of the
bulky cameraman, but then he dropped the camera,
and she saw one of the monsters up close. The veins
in his eyes bled a hateful red light, and spines of bone
had broken through his skin at odd angles all over
the body and were covered in gore. It was barely
recognizable as being human any longer. She saw it
for only a second before it took the cameraman's head
and slammed it through the window of the back door,
using its other appendage to rip the rest of the large
man's body away. As the man's head fell to her feet,

the look of shock and terror still visible on his face, Barbara added her own scream to the mix.

It was too much. She turned and pushed her way to the front of the ambulance, trying to block out LaVaca's terrified screams as she was devoured alive with screams of her own. She was a law abiding woman, she was a good person, but she wouldn't die for these people. She could already hear the creature trying to get into the ambulance. She put the ambulance in drive and floored the gas. It didn't matter that she hit several people as she tried to get out of the parking lot and onto the street. Even if they had been uninjured before she hit them, they were dead, hitting them was a mercy. It was a less horrible death than the one those things would give them.

***

Carl Northrup stood in the shadow of the apartment building. Even in the early morning sun he could see the glow coming from his veins. He rubbed his face with thirteen webbed fingers and traced the hinge of his disjointed jaw. He was so scared. He wasn't scared of the glowing veins. Or the way his skin bulged in new places and tore to let out spines. That didn't matter. Neither did all the extra teeth. No, what mattered was all the other things, things that were shaped like him. Dimly, he remembered that they were people, that he was a person. But that didn't make sense; he was different, they smelled different, and they screamed when he came near, they attacked him. They were predators, and he had to defend himself. Blood, not his, burbled in his throat as he watched a large "person" walk into the apartment building. What was he doing?

Was this a hive of "persons"? What if he was going to gather more persons, and those persons attacked him? No. No no no no no no no … Carl couldn't let that happen, he had to stop them before they … before they could hunt him down and eat him!

He almost made a sound, he almost roared his challenge, but he stopped himself in time. He wanted to surprise the persons. He wanted to get in there and kill them all before they could kill him. So instead, he silently pushed through the doors of the apartment complex and got started.

***

She had stolen an ambulance. She had stolen an ambulance and killed people fleeing the massacre outside the clinic. For the second time in as many hours, she was the only survivor of an attack by ... by what? Junkies? Addicts? She hadn't recognized the shambling masses of bone and muscle, but if they were like Carl Northrup, it had to be some sort of methamphetamine that was causing these attacks. She wanted to get away from this part of town; the farther from the methadone clinic she got, the less likely she would be surrounded by drug addled monsters. At least, that was her hope.

The ambulance handled like a child's wooden toy: capable of speed but too heavy and bulky to make tight maneuvers. On the bright side, most cars were getting out of her way, unwilling to be in front of a speeding ambulance with its lights on. Most cars. But as she drove, she saw more and more signs of panic and destruction. She saw more of the creatures too. They were attacking anything that came close to them. Two swarmed over an overturned car trying to get to the people inside.

She didn't stop. She saw people running towards the ambulance, holding wounded children or loved ones in their hands. She didn't stop. They were already dead. Despite every minute of her life being spent in health care, soaking up all the praise her friends and family lavished on her for helping people and being a saint, she didn't stop. At the end of the day, she didn't care about these people. She didn't care that they were dying, murdered by monsters that were human and inhuman all at once. The only thing she did care about was not being one of the torn apart masses now choking the streets. She laid on the horn, desperate to get those running in the middle of the street out of the way. How were there so many of these things? Where did they come from? One moment the world had been exactly as it always been, a shitty hell hole filled with shitty people treating each other like shit. But now the hell hole was filled with literal demons. In the space of a couple of hours, things had gone from normal to complete chaos, and she was adding to it.

The scream of the ambulance's sirens drowned out all the other noise. Barbara was glad for that. People were shouting over the radio in the ambulance, asking what was happening. Occasionally, a voice would cut in trying to appeal to "whoever stole the ambulance," but she ignored that. Going back towards the city center would only bring her face to face with even more of the things. Altruism was only worthwhile when it didn't get you killed. She was going to escape this. She wouldn't die for these people, not for addicts, not for doctors, not for any of the huddled masses she had been invisible to for so long. She had been forced to fight and struggle every day of her life on her own, now these leeches could see what it was like. The longer she drove and ignored the hysteria going on outside the ambulance, the more justified she felt. She considered stopping somewhere, getting a weapon, but she had seen how ineffectual weapons were first hand. No, the best thing to do was get the fuck out of San Antonio and wait it out in the rural areas while the cops dealt with this.

The radio was nonstop now.

"We have paramedics down on Babcock!"

"Is anyone near Navarro and Commerce? We have another attack!" That was downtown, that was where things would get truly dangerous.

And then there was the screaming. Just screaming. Barbara wished they would stop. What good would screaming into the radio do? They were already dead. She pushed the accelerator down and was heading for the on-ramp of 410 when a woman stumbled out of the apartment building there clutching a bleeding child to her chest and stumbled into the street directly in front of Barbara. Instinct more than a desire to spare the woman caused Barbara to swerve away from the woman. The top heavy, bulky ambulance toppled, unable to handle the sudden change in momentum. Medical supplies went everywhere, spinning within the ambulance as it rolled several feet and came to a stop.

Barbara hadn't buckled herself in, she had been too focused on fleeing, and now she lay in the overturned ambulance against a broken window, her own body refusing to respond to her brain's frantic pleas to get up and get out of there. She had to keep moving. She could barely see past the blood dripping into her eye from where her head had impacted the windshield during the wreck. She begged her arms and legs to respond.

She could hear it. That inhuman discordant scream was getting closer.

***

Carl had cleared out most of the nest. This could be his nest now. He dragged the bodies of the persons into a heap and then burrowed into it. Meat and the smell of the rot should hide his own scent. Anyone who came in would see only the dead and assume there was no hunting here. This was a good strategy. Carl had torn the persons apart on multiple levels. He could still hear more of them within the building. But that was good; if he hunted them all, it might attract other predators. Carl twitched at the thought. He would defend his new home.

An arm, a new arm, one that hadn't been there hours ago, reached out with three webbed fingers ending in sharp talons to pull an arm from the pile so he could bite into it. He didn't chew, his teeth weren't designed for that anymore. Carl simply tore off chunks of quivering cold dead meat and swallowed it whole. Shelter, food … there was something else he needed. There was another imperative. Something else.

His tongue snaked out from between rows of asymmetrical teeth to lick one eye and then the other. It left behind streaks of jellied blood, but without lids, his eyes had to stay moist this way.

***

Barbara prayed for the strength to move. When she looked up, screaming pain cycled through her entire body, a shrill note of agony from the tips of her toes to her scalp, which itched with embedded gravel from the asphalt of the roads. She looked up again, almost relishing the pain. The fact that she could feel her limbs at all was a comfort, but the world that greeted her eyes was not.

The world was on fire. At least this neighborhood was. She hadn't even made it out of the shitty drug infested dens of her clinic's zip code before crashing. She could feel the screaming of those things. They had been human. She knew that. They HAD been human. Now they were something else entirely, something horrifying and evil. She looked down, unable to keep her eyes on the burning buildings or blood streaked doors that were so close. She needed to move, she needed to get out of here. And if she was going to do that, she needed to not be in pain.

Barbara pulled herself back towards the ambulance. She could move her legs, they hurt like someone had cut her open, shoved broken glass into the muscle, and sewed her back up, but she could move them. She dragged herself, only pushing with her legs when she absolutely had to. She made it to the back of the ambulance after several grueling minutes of agonized struggle. She searched the shelves and drawers of the overturned vehicle, frantically looking for any of their painkillers. Fentanyl, morphine, and Toradol. Toradol would be the best right now, after all, it wouldn't make her drowsy, but on the other hand, she would need a lot of it to really kill the sharp shards of pain that were shooting into her every moment. The fentanyl would kill the pain, it would kill it to the point where she would be able to walk on two broken legs if she had to. If she were being honest, she might have to. She grabbed the single use injection vial and pressed it against her arm. She would grab a small canister of oxygen too ... just in case.

Just in case she had a severe respiratory depression? She was damned if she did this, she would get caught by the things out there and ripped to shreds, but if she didn't do this, she would just be a sitting duck until one of them found her anyway. She closed her eyes and pulled the trigger, injecting herself. The effect was immediate. Almost cartoonishly so. In the back of her head, the thought swam that perhaps the addicts had the right idea after all. She stood shakily and shook her head to clear it. She couldn't feel her legs, but they were moving the way she wanted them to. This was good, good enough. She stared down, noticing that she could see her veins. They seemed to emit a strange throbbing light. She was annoyed for a moment; there shouldn't be any hallucinatory side effects of fentanyl. She looked away, promising herself to just ignore it until it went away.

Stepping from the back of the toppled ambulance, Barbara completely forgot to grab oxygen, but that was okay. She looked back, looking into the ambulance; she knew there was something she needed. Something, but she couldn't bring herself to remember. The world swam in and out of focus, and with each thrum, a wave of pain washed up on the shores of her awareness. But pain was somehow new, a different sensation that wasn't all that terrible. As each wave of pain retreated, it took a bit more of her with it. Eroded the shore of who Barbara was, taking with it the fear, common sense, and will power that made up the core of who she was.

She was out in the open. She heard the shrill cry followed by the wet ripping sound of flesh being torn in places it wasn't supposed to tear. She needed to find shelter, find safety. And food. With a start, she realized she was hungry. Food and shelter. She needed to find both. And something else, there was a third thing, but for the life of her, she couldn't think of what that was.

***

Mike had called the police after finding Abby. They had told him to stay put, that someone would come as quickly as possible, but that there was major unrest in the city and it might be a while. Mike hadn't heard about any unrest, well none here anyway. Sure, there were riots and militias in other cities. Austin was a shit hole. But here? In San Antonio? When he checked the news on his phone, his heart sank. The city was besieged by what they were calling "monsters" and "creatures." But Mike knew they were just people. Just humans who had changed. Maybe some disease or weapon. Was he infected? Laura had hurt him. Badly. He was bandaged up now, but the pain was excruciating; was he also sick? Would he change and attack Abby? He took one of Laura's pain pills to take the edge off, just enough so he could protect his family.

37

They couldn't stay in the house. How could they when Laura's body was there? His wife, Abby's mother, he didn't want Abby seeing what she had become; he didn't know how to answer when Abby asked where her Mommy was. Mike assumed it was some sort of disease, some offshoot of the pandemic that had mutated beyond what scientists could have ever foreseen. But the only thing he knew for sure was that he had killed her, he had shot the woman he loved, and the mother of his child was dead in their bedroom.

And the worst part was he didn't feel sorrow. He hardly felt anything. Of course, he was afraid, afraid there were more of these things out there in San Antonio. He was terrified he had been infected. But for the death of his wife? He felt … just … relief. He felt relieved that he wouldn't have to listen to her complaining about needing the painkillers when she wasn't on them and deal with her high in front of their child when she was. He was relieved he wouldn't be trapped in a loveless, affectionless, sexless marriage where most of his time was spent trying to get his wife to care about anything other than herself.

He didn't feel sad that she was dead, and the guilt he felt over that was a physical, painful thing. His selfishness astounded him. He hurt terribly, possibly infected and dying while the city burned with monstrously changed people who were murdering, rampaging, and eating others. And all he could think about was getting back into the dating world? Mike was disgusted with himself, so he tried to focus on the one thing he knew he could do well.

"Come on, Abby, we're going."

"Where's Mommy?"

"Mommy is ..." Mike stumbled over the words. He needed Abby to be calm right now; the world was too scary as it was, and he needed to be able to protect and soothe her. "Mommy is sick, so she's resting," he finally lied. Another stab of guilt.

He set her in front of the TV and put a cartoon about friendly horses on Netflix before running back into the bedroom to grab their bugout bag. Mike wasn't a prepper, but when things had started heating up politically, especially in purple states like Texas with huge rural populations, Mike had put together a couple of bags, just in case. He was happy he had. He stepped around the still corpse of his wife. Now that he wasn't trying to staunch his bleeding or find his daughter, he took a moment to really look at her.

He could see her, make out features that were undeniably his wife's. Now that she wasn't twisted up in an inhuman hunger, she almost looked like herself. But the bullets he had fired into her had ruined any chance at a peaceful repose. Most of her jaw was missing, as was the top of her head. Her brain matter that hadn't been plastered across the ceiling pooled around the shattered edge of her skull, and her eyes bugged out of her head, almost completely red with broken capillaries. Even with all the brutality done, she still looked like Laura, less terrifying, less monstrous. At least her face did.

Her limbs were elongated, with joints in weird places, bent in ways that made his stomach turn. Bits of bone that looked like horny growths had sprouted

39

across her body with such speed and force they had torn the skin open and splattered blood around the wound. How did change like this happen so suddenly? How did a woman go from human to monster in the amount of time it took to cook a hot dog? He stood staring at the body that was once a woman he had walked down the aisle with, once thought he would die for. Grief hit him then, not for the thing that lay dead there, but for the woman he had loved, who had died years ago, murdered by pills. Taking a deep breath, Mike grabbed the bags filled with survival supplies, clothes, and other tools. Mike had been an Eagle Scout as a kid and had loved hiking and camping before Abby was born. It had been a thing Laura had loved too. Time to share it with Abby.

"Abby baby! Let's go, we're going camping while Mommy stays home!" Mike called, hurrying back into the living room, grabbing Abby's hand, and hurrying her out the door.

"But, Daddy, the TV is still on. Can't I say goodbye to Mommy?" Abby asked resisting his pull.

"Mommy's asleep" Mike muttered, wishing he could tell her the truth or say anything that wouldn't be completely devastating to his daughter.

"Oh." There was a disappointment in that. Abby didn't understand her mother's addiction. But she understood that over the last two years, Laura had stopped playing with her, stopped cooking, stopped doing anything that resembled motherhood. She understood that when Mike said that Mommy was sleeping, it meant she had taken her medicine and didn't want to be bothered.

As Mike shoved the bags into the trunk of the family Subaru, he wondered what Abby would remember of Laura. Would she remember the first 4 years when she had been a loving, kind, and outgoing mother? It was just as likely, Mike had to admit, that Abby would only remember what her mother was like after the accident, after she had gotten hooked on Vicodin. That broke his heart more than anything else. Abby would never know the woman he had fallen in love with. The mother she had been.

Mike buckled Abby into her booster seat and got behind the wheel, started the car, and then realized he had no idea where he was going.

Chapter 3

Lisa and Ferdinand stood outside of their SUV in silence. Back at the river bank, the rest of their team, interns and laborers, were breaking down their tents and portable labs while the two researchers had loaded up the specimens and started the long drive across the Texas border towards the coast. That had been the plan, anyway. Just outside of George West, they had stopped.

"Terrorists?" Lisa finally asked, as though Ferdinand might have an answer.

"Terrorists?" he echoed, looking at her with a raised eyebrow. "What kind of terrorists would attack ..." He gestured at the town, which seemed made up of two or three roads at most.

"I don't know, Freddy! But look at it!" She jutted her chin at the town, or rather what was left of it.

George West was a small town of only 2500 people or so, but if he had to guess, there weren't that many left. The small town was in flames. Large clouds of black smoke hung over the town, practically the only proof it had existed other than the rubble.

"Cartel and militia maybe?" Ferdinand finally suggested. RPGs could cause this much damage ... if they were used on every single building, multiple times. But the only other explanation he could come up with was that someone had carpet bombed the ever living fuck out of a podunk nowhere town deep in the boonies of the Lone Star State. He checked his phone for the 6th time since getting out of the car. Zero bars. It wasn't entirely surprising, he couldn't see a structure taller than a tree standing, which meant the closest cell towers had probably been flattened. He moved back to the car. "We can't do anything from here. Let's drive into town and see if there are any survivors, then we can get to the nearest place with cell service and call ..."

He trailed off. Who the fuck did you call in cases like this? It wasn't like the National Guard or the FBI had some sort of public number they could call. He supposed at the next town they could call the sheriff's office and at least report it, get news traveling up the chain. It was surreal to see destruction on this scale, and he was at a loss. So instead, he pushed it down and sat down behind the wheel, waiting for Lisa to join him. As he waited, he admired her profile. Her black skin contrasted with her red and gold shirt beautifully. She always cut an imposing figure to him, even when they were younger, meeting for the first time at conferences. His hand lifted, and he traced the scar that marred his face. It still ached when it got cold, and he had a regimen of skin creams he had to use on a nightly basis. His mother had sometimes teased him about not going into a field where he could afford plastic surgery, but he was proud of who he was, even if it was a lonely life.

"Okay, so let's see if we can find survivors ..." Lisa said as she finally got back in the car.

He didn't argue, just drove into what remained of the town. There wasn't much of a town to drive through even before this destruction laid it low. He could only guess that they were near what had once been the town hall when they saw movement. Lisa spotted it first as Ferdinand maneuvered the SUV around debris in the road.

"There's someone!" she nearly shouted, causing him to jump.

He swallowed his irritation and followed her pointing finger to a nearby collapsed store front. Sure enough, there was a figure stumbling out of the rubble. He stopped the car, ready to jump out. It was obvious the person's legs were in bad shape from their shuffling gait.

"Wait, there's more survivors," Lisa stuttered before he could unbuckle his seatbelt.

There were. A dozen or so shapes were emerging from within the destroyed buildings, probably drawn out by the sound of the car. As they emerged from the heavy smoke that covered most the town, it became apparent their injuries were disastrously severe. Limbs sat at unnatural angles, and jaws were set askew from the rest of the head. Blood seeped from eyes and fresh wounds on every person he could see, but there was something else.

There was something unnatural about them. They moved with the sloppy walk of a water animal on land, not the limp of someone injured, and what he had taken to be shrapnel or bones broken and sticking from torn flesh at first now looked like spines and claws. He was about to turn to suggest something was off to Lisa when they heard a bone shaking scream that echoed throughout the small town. It was answered by a hundred more screams. Ferdinand turned to Lisa to formulate a thought, and so he had a small warning when he saw the man, or what was once a man, on the other side of her window.

Less than a second later, the window shattered and the man was scrabbling to get inside the car with them.

"Fuck!" Ferdinand slammed on the gas, trying to dislodge the attacker, his eyes checking the road one moment and the situation in his passenger seat the next. He checked the rear view and saw that while the things were chasing them faster than any natural man could hope to, they still fell behind. One of the attackers' hands was on the dashboard. It had seven fingers, and the fingers had too many joints, each topped with a spur of bone that glistened with some slimy substance. He realized he could see the man's pulse through his skin, a reddish glow that brightened with every heartbeat. Another hand was on the inside of the car trying to maintain a grip and provide leverage. A third arm, this one with no claws, talons, or fingers at all, but a fleshy lump, was clubbing at Lisa.

Glancing up at the road to check for immediate debris as they shot forward, Ferdinand darted past the grasping clawed hand, earning deep scratches from the bone spurs as he popped the glove compartment and retrieved his handgun. Flipping the safety off, he glanced back at the road; they were already out of the town. He fired three shots, aiming for the center mass of the man. It howled, opening its mouth too far to reveal rows of curved teeth that looked perfect for tearing through chunks of meat. He didn't hesitate, worried more for Lisa than himself. He jammed the gun down the man's throat and fired off three more shots. The back of the creature's head exploded, and it tumbled back and out of the car, catching the road and falling still. Glowing blood filled the car, swiftly dimming to a dull blackish red. He looked back in the rear view, hoping the thing was actually dead and there would be no other things catching up.

He was so concerned with what was happening behind him that it wasn't until Lisa began screaming that he wrenched his head back towards the road and saw the bridge over the nearby Nueces River had been torn apart. Not just destroyed, but savaged, as though some immense beast had taken it and twisted it into strange and broken shapes. An image that did not sit easily with Ferdinand as he caught a glimpse of what looked like massive claws marks on the Nueces's far shore. What could have possibly done this? What connection did it have to the freakishly mutated monster that had attacked the car?

"We have to turn around," Lisa said finally.

"Are you insane? You saw those things, you saw ..." Ferdinand gestured helplessly to the inside of the car where the creature's blood and claw marks had left extensive damage to the interior.

"So we just sit here?" she spat back, the fear making her irritable. "No, we need turn back and find some way around this."

Ferdinand nodded and turned them around, heading back down the road into town. "We can head north on 281 towards San Antonio. There are lots of military there. It's a big city. Someone there will be able to help us."

It seemed like a decent enough plan, but in the back of his mind, Ferdinand was awash with fear. What would happen when he got back into town and they were surrounded by those things? Would they be able to outrun and outmaneuver whatever those things were? And even if they did, even if they were able to get past this town and the monsters that inhabited it, would they make it to San Antonio without getting gas? How far north did this destruction go? Would San Antonio be in a similar condition? And from the claw marks he had seen at the river, whatever had destroyed the bridge was also heading north ...

As they approached the town, Ferdinand pressed the gas a little harder, hoping he could make it through before any of those things came out. No such luck, but it seemed the malformed creatures weren't fast enough to keep up with the car, and most gave up and turned back at the edge of the ruined town.

"They're the same," Lisa murmured, watching the monsters fade into the background.

"What?"

"They're the same as the siren, as the salamanders

47

we saw. It's the same mutation," she responded, her eyes moving to the back of the SUV where the tank with the specimen sat in relative peace, unperturbed by the violence surrounding it.

"You think ... Lisa, mutations don't work like that. It happens on a generational scale."

"I'm sorry, Dr. Sila, but are you trying to explain evolution and mutation to me?"

Ferdinand shut up. Lisa was a brilliant scientist; he shouldn't dismiss her theories simply because he didn't understand them.

"Okay ... I'm sorry. What do you mean?"

"The glowing blood. That ... thing was producing luciferins, in the blood, just like the salamander. You can't think that's a coincidence." She shot him a look, daring him to try to argue with her.

He wisely stayed silent. He wanted to know what she was thinking, but at the same time, he wanted his arm, where it had been scraped against the bony spins of the creature's hands, to stop hurting.

"So, if it isn't a coincidence, what is causing these things to mutate like this?" Lisa finished.

Ferdinand turned the question over in his head. It was a conundrum. "When we get to San Antonio, we can take a closer look at the specimens we've gathered and ..." he trailed off, realizing their team would be heading straight into the town, straight towards the missing bridge and the monsters that hid in the debris of the destruction. Without finishing his thought, he pushed the gas a little harder, praying they could reach cell service before their team lost theirs.

***

The fog rolled into Three Rivers, Texas in the late afternoon. This in and of itself would be enough to alarm the citizens of the tiny Texas town, but the Earth was shaking. Not shaking like an earthquake, not that anyone born and raised in a town whose biggest attraction was its very own city pool would know what an earthquake felt like.

Jay stared at the paper cup of coffee on the table, watching the ripples. His immediate thought was that this was just like that one scene in the Jurassic park movie. The earth shaking was rhythmic, like one of the kids was playing some bass heavy hip-hop on a speaker that they had decided to point directly into the ground.

Jay wondered about it for a long moment. He wasn't overly worried. He was still nursing his hangover, sitting in the Three Rivers Donuts/Chinese Food; the coffee sucked, but it was a getaway from listening to his in-laws bitch about various things that didn't matter. It wasn't until someone else started yammering and shouting that Jay looked up.

"Martha, calm down, it's just ..." Jay trailed off. It was just what? A dinosaur? No, it was just ... something. "It's probably just road construction crews or something." Two highways and three rivers, that's all the bullshit town was. When he had first been discharged from the army, the thought of a small town where everyone knew everyone had sounded nice. It was a good plan, away from the violence of the big city to raise his kids. Now he hated every fucking second of it. He lifted his eyes so he could look the older woman in the face and try to be reassuring. It wasn't her fault this town was such horse shit. She was just a woman struggling to do her best like everyone else. He was about to offer another explanation for the noise, his hangover addled brain lagging behind his good intentions, when he stopped. A red fog was rolling over the town.

Jay wondered if it were a fog or a mist. The stray thoughts and non-sequential abstracts that flowed into his brain frustrated him. It was like when he got into a fight with his mother-in-law, and while she was standing there reaming him out, all he could think about was old cartoons of Ren and Stimpy. She was a chihuahua of a woman, and he was the fat cat who couldn't do anything right in her eyes.

Martha was opening the door to the little donut shop, trying to investigate, too damn curious. As soon as the door was open, the red mist enveloped her, pouring into the restaurant in slow heavy waves. Martha started screaming.

Jay stood, knocking his chair backwards, and darted forward to grab the older woman. He held his breath as he hit the red mist and dragged her backwards out of it. His skin didn't burn, his eyes didn't sting. Why was Martha screaming and writhing on the floor? Jay stared down at her, unsure how to help now.

"Mother fucker!" Jay shouted, falling backwards as Martha's body began to contort, bony spines pushing their way out of the skin with enough speed to dislodge gristle and send bloody chunks of flesh across the shop. Other people were screaming now. The door was still open. There was more of the mist.

Jay pulled himself back up and was standing over the convulsing form of the woman when she suddenly stopped moving. She was still breathing, but she wasn't even human anymore. Extra limbs and strange growths covered her body. Her hand, which twitched with spasms, had nine fingers now, all ending in a talon of bone that had ripped through the nail bed. He stared down at her in shock. What the hell was that mist? Apprehensively, he looked at his own hands, looking for any inkling of the changes that had wracked Martha. He thought he saw a dim glow of red from the veins in his hand, but it was so dim it could be his imagination.

Martha let out a sudden groan.

"Jesus fuck!" Jay shouted, jumping back as the tangle of limbs and claws and spines began moving, hissing, rising from the ground. The veins in her malformed face were pulsing like the lights outside that one strip club in Dallas. Her mouth was filled with bony protrusions that looked like sharpened bits of tusk. She gurgled an awful roar and charged at Jay, swiping at him with a hand much larger than it should be. Jay acted without thinking, pulling his .45 ACP from his hip holster and flipping the safety in one smooth move, a byproduct of the copious amount of time he spent at the range, he fired at Martha, and then again and again, pumping three rounds into the woman before she dropped.

"What the hell ..." He edged forward and prodded

51

Martha's dead body with his shoe, making sure she was dead. He was so focused on that he almost missed the rattling from the other patrons of the little donut shop. He looked up when he heard a massive crash and explosion from outside. What the hell was going on? He moved to the window, trying to see through the thick red fog that was beginning to coat the town. He couldn't see much from the window other than a few people running. The massive thuds that shook the Earth were close now, so close that he felt that at any moment the world would open up and swallow him whole. He heard a scream and the sound of tearing flesh from behind him.

Turning, he saw several more of the other customers had gone through the same change as Martha, those that didn't lie in shredded piles of flesh and meat. Pools of blood and less savory fluids spread across the floor, reaching for Jay even as the monsters the patrons had become did the same. With a snarl, Jay lifted his gun and fired, no warning shots. The pussies in the Army may believe in warning shots, but he would be triple fucked if he let one of these damn monsters lay a mutated finger on him. He kept shooting, calmly aiming for the heads. Five shots later and the monsters were dead. Bits of bone and flesh torn apart by the large caliber bullets Jay would swear by 'til the day he died.

Jay moved to the counter and leapt over, glancing through the serving window into the kitchen. The back door hung off its hinges, and there were several dead bodies. Whatever the mist was turning people into, they were killing indiscriminately.

There was another massive explosion from outside.

Jay couldn't stay here, he needed to get more ammo, and after a second's thought, to get to his family and protect them, get them somewhere they could defend against these monsters. He checked his cell phone, a bunch of missed calls and texts from his wife, but now, now there was no service. He noticed the butt of a shotgun under the counter. That could be useful. He holstered his .45, empty now anyway, and grabbed the shotgun, taking a moment to look it over. It seemed to be in good working order. He opened a few drawers until he found a box of shells and shoved that into a small to-go bag that was sitting on the counter. The entire time, the earth shook and explosions and crashes continued.

Jay was armed better now. He felt confident; even if he had been kicked out of the Army, he was still a trained killer, no mutated monster fucks were going to get him. Not when he was armed. He just needed to get to his truck and get back to the house to pick up his wife and kids—in-laws could get fucked—and get the hell out of here. He moved across the donut shop again, squelching through the remains of friends and acquaintances. The death didn't bother him, the carnage didn't worry him. He was in his element, he was John Rambo, he was Snake Plissken, Neo, Mad Max, Henry Callahan. He was the quintessential bad ass.

He kicked open the door and charged out, swinging the barrel of the shotgun around, looking for targets, daring any of these monster assholes to come at him. The earth shook so hard he nearly lost his footing. The sound of a building being demolished crashed through him. Dust and debris flew through the air, a chunk of masonry clipping Jay in the head, dropping him like a sack filled with lead. He struggled to his feet, blood dripping into his eyes. He reached up woozily to wipe away as much of the blood as he could. The world was still red; the mist, the blood, the pain, the world was red. Something took shape in the fog coming toward him, something larger than anything else in Three Rivers.

It towered over the buildings surrounding it, a massive flat head that slowly turned as if surveying its land. The thing was white, or slightly translucent, and Jay could see the pulsing light of its circulatory system thrumming as it took another ponderous step towards him. The entire world shook. It stood awkwardly, hunched over on two legs that carried it above the world, ending in claws that could crush busses. Each claw had four toes, and each toe was tipped with a claw that looked perfectly capable of ripping another creature apart, though what creature this thing would be fighting was anyone's guess. As it emerged from the fog, Jay saw it was a long creature, the majority of its mass hidden within the red clouds that had mutated the people of Three Rivers. Its long flat head was flanked on both sides by prongs of flesh sporting brightly glowing red fronds that waved and vibrated in the air. It looked like some massive slimy lizard wearing one of those headdresses he saw women in bikinis wearing while they danced on the streets of Brazil during Carnival. Jay didn't know what a salamander was, sure as fuck had never heard of an axolotl.

The massive black eyes, like buttons just above the wide flat mouth, showed no emotion. No rage, no purpose, not even a hint of malevolence. It just peered at the world as though confused by everything it was destroying. And it was destroying everything. Behind it, fires raged. Those things not torn down by its footsteps were swept aside by the sweep of its tale.

Jay looked down at his shotgun; this wasn't going to be good enough. Luckily, he knew that if he got to 3Rivers Ammo, he could restock on ammo and probably grab a better weapon, maybe team up with some of the guys from the range. He turned and ran, but he wasn't running from the creature. No, he screamed in his own mind, other people ran from this, he was running to a fight, getting to somewhere he could defend.

As he rounded the street, he saw a band of those mutated monsters. Things that had been people before the red mist had taken them and turned them into these grasping and gasping things. Jay wished he had solid slugs instead of buckshot, but beggars couldn't be choosers. So instead of wasting time lamenting his options or trying to guess who these people had been, Jay lifted the shotgun to his shoulder and fired, spraying the three monsters with enough death to take down a group of humans. They didn't go down. They shrieked, their misshapen bodies moving painfully, as though the spines and bones had grown and fused with no consideration for how the body would function after. He let fly with the other barrel. There was only so much damage these monsters could take.

Jay broke open the shotgun, loading two more shells. He was feeling confident. The giant lizard had to be a mutant created by the red mist. And if these creatures laying dying at his feet could be taken out with buckshot, it meant the lizard could be killed too. He just needed a big enough gun. Jay smiled as he charged down the street, looking for more monsters to kill. That would be his quote when he was rewarded. He could see it now, the President draping a medal over his neck, everyone in awe of Jay, women throwing themselves at him as the savior of Texas, no, fuck that, probably the world. He would tell his story, and he would say, "And I said, looks like we're going to need a bigger gun." And the cleverness of his retort would skyrocket his fame to the point he would literally drown in pussy and fake tits. In fact, he would probably get ...

Jay screamed as he lost a leg but kept his forward momentum.

Blood pumped freely from the torn and ruined hole that used to end in a leg. The creature that had taken it used to be a child. It was too small to be an adult, but that was his only indication that it had ever been human at all. It was tearing into his leg, eating it, long tusks tearing flesh out of the separated limb and gulping it down. Still screaming, Jay lifted the shotgun, trying to aim as best he could, when a second bony talon slammed through his shoulder. His screams echoed through the town, even louder than the destruction, as another creature, still wearing its good Sunday dress, leaned over him and began tearing into his face to take long hungry gulps of cheek meat.

Above them, the axolotl roared, oblivious to the carnage below, copious thick red mist pouring from its maw.

John Baltisberger

Chapter 4

Barbara walked the streets of San Antonio. She wasn't walking right either. Her leg dragged a bit. The drugs flooding her system let her ignore it. Maybe it hurt? She couldn't tell if it hurt, the pain was too far away, out of grasp. Silently, she cursed taking the fentanyl, it was making it too hard to think. Her brain wouldn't fire correctly, and every few moments, she had to try to remember where she was going. Where was she going?

She stood in the middle of the street, staring off into the distance. A glob of drool mixed with thick, glowing blood dripped from the corner of her mouth, from between teeth that had begun to jut out. She knew they were jutting out because she had bitten her lip several times. It was annoying, but didn't hurt too much. The fourth time it happened, it had aggravated her so much that she had gone to work on it, scraping her bottom teeth up over the lip and dragging them down, working until she had succeeded in tearing her upper lip off. She had eaten it; no sense in letting it go to waste after all, she was hungry.

She glanced back at her leg that was dragging behind her. It didn't make sense. That leg had two feet. Of course, one foot dangled uselessly, the dewclaw twitching slightly. But still, with two feet, that leg ought to work better. She snorted and started to say something but bit her bottom lip. With a feral roar of frustration, Barbara reached up and used the talons that had pushed their way through her nail bed to shred the skin there. It was a distraction. Once the skin had been flayed from her lower jaw, she greedily slurped the meat from her talons, then took a moment to look at her fingers. They hadn't always been like that, had they? Somewhere deep in the back of her mind, she remembered getting a manicure. She had gotten them done all up in green with darker green tips. These were red. She stared silently, listening to the sound of air being brought into her lungs and then pushed out of her gills. Something wasn't right with her nails. But she liked the red, it was pretty.

A scream split the air. Barbara spun and spotted a family, two adults and a child. They were pointing at her and being loud. Barbara took a step back; she could run, she should run. But what if ... what if that scream attracted more of them and they chased her? Maybe she could convince them she wasn't a threat. She took several steps towards the family, raising her claws and jabbering. Without lips and with two tongues, the sounds coming from her throat didn't form words. Not the words she meant. They were hisses and howls. But she hoped they would understand none the less.

They didn't.

They started running.

59

No!

Barbara dropped to all five and started chasing them. They couldn't go back to their nest and bring more fierce protectors. She didn't want to hurt them, she wanted to be left alone, but she couldn't let the threat survive.

She leapt.

The child crunched under her, its body convulsed, and a quick look told her its head was leaking blood and something meaty onto the ground. Thoughts of protecting herself began to seep away. Her stomach was knotted with how hungry she was. She reached down to scoop up a bit of the grayish pink meat that spilled out, eager to taste it. But she was interrupted when something barreled into her.

The male ...

The male was screaming at her; it wanted to eat the young she had killed!

Well that wasn't happening. She roared a challenge, scrambling forward on a mess of limbs and talons. She wanted more of the gray meat. Her leg kicked out, the razor-sharp talons on her extra foot flailing and severing the man's leg just below the knee. But rather than let him fall to the ground, her left hand, (was it always that big?) caught him by the head and slammed it into the nearby wall. It cracked, but it was harder than the child. The male still muttered and mumbled. One eye had been dislodged, it hung limply from a chord, the other rolled uselessly. She needed to hit harder. Or she needed more momentum!

She pulled back from the wall and scurried forward as fast as she could to slam his head into the wall again. The dangling eye bounced on its nerves before getting caught between the wall and the man's head, exploding on impact. The man screamed, but it wasn't a coherent scream. It was the scream of a man whose brain had been irrevocably damaged. It started loud and sure, quickly losing power and volume as he succumbed to the abyss of shock. Frustrated once more, Barbara decided to go back on a tried and true method. She pushed the man down and tore at his mouth with her teeth. She would go up through the soft palate.

The female was screaming, screaming so loud that normally Barbara would be worried about other predators. But she had just defended a meal. No! She had doubled a meal, and she felt invincible. Let the female scream. Barbara would continue to slurp up the slurry of nearly liquefied brain meat from the male's head, and when she was done with that, she would feast on the child. But even then, she knew she still needed shelter, shelter and something else.

***

The screaming from the woman did attract attention. Barbara looked up, drenched in gore from her meal. It was almost too much; her stomach was distended from the meat and gristle of the adult male. It popped out from under her shredded top and over what remained of her pants. More of the people were showing up, people ... she was a people, a person. Barbara shook her head, the shattered remains of her psyche recoiling in horror from what she had done.

She tried to cry out in fear, she tried to explain that she didn't know what happened, but the words wouldn't form around her bone tusks without the help of lips. She remembered tearing her own lips off and wailed in terror. The drugs, this was all a hallucination brought on by drugs.

She looked down at the grisly remains at her feet. It wasn't recognizable. Her stomach lurched. She was sickened by what she had done, but not by the flavor of the family's flesh and organs. She could still taste it on her tongues, and it tasted heavenly. She wanted to run, but she was surrounded, people were coming at her. She was one of them! They couldn't kill her! But she knew they would. What she had done was unforgivable. But she had just been defending herself. She had just been hungry. She knew she couldn't reason with these things; they were selfish and angry, they would attack her despite the loss of just a few of them not being impactful for the whole. Over their heads she saw flashing blue and red lights. Instinctively, she knew this would be their warriors. The most dangerous these things had. Barbara knew she had to do something fast. Lamenting the loss of her meal, Barbara vomited. Ejecting barely masticated flesh and organs, still recognizable for her lack of chewing, onto the ground.

The people panicked at that as bits of bile and bone she had accidentally swallowed while getting at marrow hit the pavement. Her stomach shrank back to a normal size, though it had loose folds to store food when she was in a position to safely eat again.

Screams erupted from the other side of the crowd. Barbara couldn't see anything, but the musk hit her, a male. A male was coming to save her. She lifted her head and screamed into the air triumphantly, a discordant note that ripped through the minds of the gathering throng, a throng that was now moving like a tide to get away from not one but two monstrosities. Barbara didn't care, she knew she had the advantage now. She surged forward, intent on doing as much damage to the human swarm as she could. If she killed enough, perhaps this hive would perish, or at least be too weak to retaliate.

Through the constant press of flesh around her, Barbara caught sight of her knight in shining armor. His arms were massive, swinging and crushing any human too slow to avoid his charge. His lower jaw was a mess of teeth that jutted out past his face, giving him an almost bulldozer appearance. And all three of his eyes were solid black, reflecting the carnage around him. Shards of jagged bone protruded at odd angles from his back and head, and each hand ended in at least ten talon tipped digits.

Barbara realized with sudden and stark clarity as she watched this new male wade into the carnage that they were creating what was missing. In that moment, as he tore a woman's core out and bit through another man's shoulder, pulling the muscle and bone beneath, she ached. The cold hollowness in her abdomen gave her a clear indication. She needed a male that could protect them, that could hunt and provide food, shelter, and the something else.

The blood and noise attracted attention, not just from the human police, but from more and more of the afflicted. Men and women whose bodies had been torn apart and reformed into glorious testaments to evolutionary superiority. They were vibrant, glowing with the internal light of bio-luminescence, painting the street red as they gathered in large numbers. The scent of human blood, of fresh meat was a siren call they could not ignore. They were solitary, gathering in a frenzy of crooked tusks and inward facing teeth. The screams and cries of the creatures who had once been men shook the windows of the nearby buildings.

The police fled too. Not the initial officers who had responded, they had been killed quickly, trampled by the human stampede of fear that cracked their skulls against the pavement and fled without a single thought to those left behind or underfoot. The police fled back to their precinct, barring doors, grabbing shotguns. They would protect themselves, watch each other's backs, let the populace tear itself apart. It wasn't until the blood started pouring under the doorway from a backroom that they realized not all the screams were coming from outside the precinct.

The streets there in Central San Antonio belonged to them now. They swarmed, leaving a trail of organs and severed, mutilated body parts in their wake. Several holed up in nearby apartments and buildings, creating filthy nests out of the discarded ribs and viscera. The Texas sun baked the gore into the pavement, but Barbara was on a mission. She slinked through the shadows and in between buildings on her way through the city. She knew what she needed, and deep inside her brain, shifting neural pathways demanded she seek it out.

***

Owen Braunfels sat in his kitchen, sipping a Shiner and watching the news. The news was insane. For a few minutes, Owen thought maybe someone was playing a joke on him. Then thought maybe this was just more leftist rioting going on again. But it had never been this bad before. People were being ripped apart. Even from the news copter, everything looked fucked up. Downtown was on fire. Owen tipped his beer again. Empty. He went and grabbed another. As he grabbed the second, no, fourth beer, he glanced at his phone. The part of town being attacked was right near where Barbara worked. He was worried about her; she was a decent girlfriend, she held down a job so he didn't have to pay for her clothes or food, she was working most the time so he was free to enjoy his own personal life, including the occasional side piece, and when she was around, she gave pretty decent head. A win-win as far as he was concerned, and he would hate to lose that easy and comfortable relationship he had built.

No texts, no calls. Owen considered calling her, maybe Barbara needed help, but at the same time, if he did call her and she was okay, she would want to bitch about work or about the chaos in the streets. She might even cry. It wasn't that he was opposed to being a shoulder to cry on. Hell, everyone needed to bitch about shit once in a while. But honestly? She was non-stop. The old joke about the reason men liking blowjobs being because it kept a woman from talking floated through his head, and he chuckled to himself. No, he could wait until they saw each other in person to listen to the whining. Then at least he could redirect it to getting dinner or watching something.

There was a thud against his door that made Owen jump. It hadn't been a knock; it had been a slam. Owen grumped and set down his beer. If any of those self-styled communists BLM protesters came to his door, he would definitely give them a good welcome. He glanced through the keyhole and immediately fell back with an alarmed cry.

It was a monster scrambling at his door.

Now that it wasn't slamming into the door, he could hear its raspy breathing. As he listened, he realized he heard something jingling. With wide eyes, he watched as the deadbolt turned and the door swung open.

The creature in front of him was a nightmare of limbs and tortured flesh, covered in gore and twisted musculature that pulsed in the low light of the apartment's hallway. Its jaw worked in horrible motion, as though mandibles were working under the skin trying to work their way free.

"Ohn. Ohn. Ohn ohn ohn ohn ohn ohn." The thing in front of him panted in a lipless thick parody of his name. Thick blood-flecked drool dripped from between its sharp broken teeth in gruesome strands. It skittered towards him with three legs, each leaving deep bloodstained grooves in the carpet as it reached for him. He could see the maroon scrubs plastered in scraps to the creature's body. He could see Barbara's keys, with their stupid fucking Hello Kitty key chain. How many times had he mocked her for that? He had wanted her to grow the fuck up, and now she had grown up into some kind of monster.

Owen scrambled back away from her and into the kitchen, grabbing the biggest knife handle he could spot in the wooden block. Spinning around to face the thing again, Owen lifted the ... bread knife.

"Get back, fucker!"

Part of his mind knew this was Barbara; he didn't know how, but it was saying his name, wearing her clothes, and had her keys. This was Barbara. That part of his brain wasn't the strongest at the best of times, and as usual, Owen fell back on pure false machismo, brandishing the knife and twirling it around in what he thought was both a cool and threatening display of skill.

Barbara watched the lackluster display, which showcased how little dexterity Owen possessed. She should eat him. He was threatening her, and she was hungry after losing her last meal in the streets to get away from the crowd. She could crack his skull open and dig through his entrails for the tastiest parts. But she wanted him. She recognized Owen, and while they hadn't had the happiest years together, they were at least familiar. It was at least something she was used to, a modicum of normalcy and control. She wanted control. She wanted to have her life back, but she couldn't remember her life. She knew there were other things she used to do when she felt like she didn't have control of a situation. She would cut her hair, get her nails done, or have an extra cheat day on her diet. Ignoring Owen's displays, Barbara reached up and touched her head. What little hair was there she tore out and looked at, each eye moving independently, allowing her to keep a watchful eye on her boyfriend and watch as the wisps of remaining hair slipped from between her gnarled, twitching fingers.

She could feel tears welling up. She needed control, but more than that, she needed to be comforted. Told she was still pretty. Told she was still precious. All five of her eyes swiveled to lock onto Owen. Her heart ached because she did care for him. He was food, a meal to make, but she couldn't bring herself to do that. She still needed the other thing: she needed a male to fertilize her, to fill her body with seed so she could give life and continue the species. Barbara had always wanted to be a mother, a dream Owen didn't share, a dream she had given up as life beat her down. But now, with biological need rewiring her brain and body for evolutionary superiority, she couldn't ignore the dream anymore. And Owen wouldn't deny her. She would prove she was the perfect mother. The perfect mate.

She gagged, she didn't know what was happening to her, but her body knew. A second gag and she vomited, but instead of the remains of her last meal, long thick strands of phlegm rocketed from her mouth and enveloped Owen. The force of the vomited phlegm tossed him into the dining room wall, where he stuck like a fly in a web. He was cocooned in the stuff, and she just kept retching more of it onto him as she moved forward. The smell was overwhelming, like rot and bile and blood. Finally, she seemed empty.

Barbara fell back against the kitchen counter, breathing hard. It had taken a lot out of her. The instinctual part of her brain understood that she needed him there, stuck to the wall. She needed him alive. He wasn't food, he was more important. But she was still a woman, she was still Barbara. Somewhere deep within her rerouted brain, she hated how Owen kept screaming in fear. She hated how he had soiled himself. She could smell it, the shit and piss mixed with the heady aroma of her phlegmy webbing. She felt the lump in her throat. She needed to prepare their nest. No, not nest, people had apartments. She needed to prepare their apartment, make it better for keeping eggs and raising babies into nymphs.

But she couldn't do it on an empty stomach. She would need to hunt and find food. Once she had eaten her fill, she could come back here, prepare the nest. But first she would comfort her screaming lover. She crept forward, pressing her warped body into the drying crust of her expunged webbing, and licked at his face. It left a trail of oozing saliva, still thick with mucus. But she knew even as he continued to scream that he would appreciate the gesture of affection. And it left her scent on him. If any other females tried to encroach on her nest and man, that would be ample warning. And if they ignored it ... well if they ignored it, she would defend what was hers as violently as she needed to.

"Ohn." She whispered as affectionately as her misshapen mouth would allow and then scuttled through the door of the apartment to find food.

***

Mike drove. He knew he needed to get out of the city. Highways were choked with traffic and cars. The city was in chaos as the sick people who had become monsters tore people and buildings apart. The smell of gunpowder and fires filled the air even out in the suburbs. Mike kept his head low, scanning the streets for cars and for any signs of more infected. It occurred to him that this was like the zombie movies he liked so much. It was less fun in real life. He struggled to think about what he knew and what he should do over the sound of his daughter singing "Kindness is Mystic" from her horse show over and over again.

He did his best to ignore her. The constant repetition combining with the pain of loss and the acrid sting of fear was overpowering. His left hand was locked on the steering wheel, his right hovering over the gun in his lap. As a general rule, he didn't like guns; he had learned to shoot with his dad, but had never really enjoyed the ammo-sexual culture that seemed to pervade the deep south. He had picked up the little Springfield 9mm during the widespread protests that had gone on a few years back. That didn't matter right now; what mattered was protecting Abby. The song she had been singing finally ended as she got bored of singing it and brought up the show on her tablet.

Another thing he wasn't a huge fan of, but he had to admit it had saved his life and sanity over the last year. Laura's addiction forced him into the role of single parent, and the tablet and streaming services acted as a babysitter when he was too busy or just needed to escape reality for a moment. Now he was grateful for the little tablet again. Her eyes would be glued to the screen and not to the world around them. Mike cruised down the streets, trying to remember the way towards the nearest camp ground. He hadn't been in years, but if he was lucky, he would be able wait out the path of this disease. He had thought about it often during the pandemic that had swept the world, *Why not just go into the country and live like hikers for a while?*

Of course, that hadn't lasted a few weeks, it had lasted almost two years. Who knew how long this would last? Again, Mike felt a pang of panic. What if he was infected? What if Abby was? His stomach twisted in pain and fear. He couldn't think about that. No, they would get out to the campgrounds and away from the urban sprawl of Texas cities.

Ahead of him, he saw a row of police cars forming a barricade across the road. He slowed down, color draining from his face. What if someone had heard the gunshots? What if they had called the police and found Laura? Mike switched hands on the wheel and moved the gun from his lap to his side so that it wouldn't be visible from the window. Sure enough, a cop approached his car, lifting a hand to order Mike to stop. Mike feigned a smile as he rolled down the window.

"Afternoon, Officer ..."

"Hello, sir, where are you headed?"

"Just going camping with my daughter. Good weather, figured I should take the chance while it isn't raining or too hot." Mike forced a laugh, hoping he didn't sound as unnatural as he felt.

"In the middle of all this?" the cop asked, raising an eyebrow. His eyes were brown and darted around the area. He knew about the sick.

"Uh, yeah, you know, I felt like it would be a good

time to get out of town, get my girl to safety."

"Uh huh, and where is the mother?" the cop asked as he bent over to look in the back seat.

"My wife, she ... she's staying with her family, she doesn't like camping," Mike finished lamely.

"What? No, she's not!" Abby called from the back seat. "She got angry and scary and then you said she was asleep!"

The cop's eyebrows shot up, and his hand fell to his waist.

Mike cursed a seven-year-old's natural honesty.

"Sir, how about you step out of the car?" The tone was forced friendly, but there wasn't any warmth in it.

Mike looked back at Abby. If they police went and checked his house, they would find the body, they would understand why he was fleeing. But would he have that chance? Would they see his gun? Hear reports of shots fired at his address? Would they just arrest him and take Abby back into a city that was teeming with monsters?

In one smooth motion, Mike brought the gun up and fired into the cop's chest. Blood splattered against Mike's face as the cop fell back. Before his body even hit the pavement, Mike slammed on the gas, gunning the car towards the biggest gap he saw in the barricade. Police were already reacting, diving out of the way, drawing their guns.

"Fuck, shit. Abby, shut up!"

In the back seat, Abby was screaming. She was terrified—first the loud sound of the gun going off, then the yelling and screaming followed by the crunchy scratching as the Subaru crashed through a barricade it just barely didn't fit through. Mike didn't let his foot off the gas. In the rear view, he could see the cops scrambling into their cars. The one he had shot was motionless, and at least two others had been injured as he forced his way through.

What was he thinking? Now not only were there monsters, but the cops were after him. And he had killed a man. He had killed two people! Mike could barely breathe, the fear reaching up from his colon to grip his throat. Why had he done that? How was this better than if he had just waited it out? Mike didn't have answers, all he had was fear. He wanted to protect his daughter, he wanted to get her away from the city, from the monsters, from corrupt police who were more concerned with the appearance of law than actually protecting them, and away from Laura's body.

He pushed his car as hard as it would go, making turns wildly in some attempt to throw the police off, but outside of town there weren't a lot of turns and roads or buildings to hide behind. As soon as he lost the lights in his line of sight, he pulled into a parking garage off of a business park just north of town. He shut off the engine and climbed into the back seat, pulling Abby to his chest and holding her.

She hadn't stopped crying, and he couldn't shake the pain that he had traumatized his daughter. He just wanted to be a good dad, he just wanted to protect his little girl. He stayed there with Abby, just holding her and whispering meaningless platitudes until she calmed down. He couldn't hear sirens anymore, but he knew it still wasn't safe. San Antonio would never be safe again. He needed to keep going north. He remembered the Cibolo Gardens nature preserve; that's where he would take Abby to wait out the chaos.

John Baltisberger

Abhorrent Siren

Chapter 5

"Freddy, let me drive," Lisa said for the fifth time. And for the fifth time, Ferdinand shook his head. He didn't even know why he was refusing at this point … well, that wasn't quite true, he was being selfish. He was fearful. He was terrified of the creatures they had seen in George West, and now he was terrified he was going to die. Driving gave him something to do, something to concentrate on other than the throbbing pain in his arm where he had scraped against the creature that attacked them.

"Fred. Ferdinand," she repeated.

Using his full name dragged his attention away from the road and to her for a moment. She looked concerned. She was a lovely person, someone who cared about others in a way that felt genuine. His eyes darted between her and the road for a moment before he finally gave in.

"Okay, okay. We're just an hour away from San Antonio; you can take the last hour." He pulled over and stretched, using the opportunity to move around to the back and pop it open to check out the specimens. And to try and call the team again. The massive axolotl floated in its tank, seeming completely at ease with its current surroundings. Ferdinand bent down to look closer at the creature. Lisa was right about how the two creatures, this one and the one that attacked them, must be related. They both glowed with their own infernal and internal light, as though their circulatory system was on fire, devouring them from the outside in. But that wasn't all.

The big axolotl in the tank had changed more since they had begun transporting it. Normally, he would have passed off something like a change a specimen as something he missed before, but there was no way he missed these changes.

"Lisa! Check this out real quick," he called, moving to lift the lids off the smaller tanks to see if there were similar changes in other animals.

Lisa rounded the back of the SUV and cried out when she saw the salamander was scratching at the tank wall with six legs, staring at her with several more eyes that each swiveled to follow her whenever she moved.

"What the hell?" she asked, approaching the tank and touching the glass. The axolotl inside frenzied, striking at her fingers and scratching at the glass, furiously trying to get at her. "This is exactly what was going on with those people we saw, the mutations, the aggressive behavior." She moved over to Ferdinand's side to look into the tank he had opened, revealing a fat frog with long articulated claws on its front legs, with which it was tearing apart the other frogs and devouring them.

"Cannibalism isn't unheard of in amphibians," he offered, his stomach unsettled by the display. He replaced the lid. "You're right, this looks to be the same thing that was happening to the people. I hate to assume, but I think it's our safest guess at this point. I also think that it doesn't change our course of action. Shit, should we try to replace the water? Maybe that's what's causing this."

Each of the tanks had been filled with water from the Rio Grande to help keep the animals safe and healthy, but what if the water itself was the issue? And on top of that, why the opium? The pieces of the puzzle were all in front of him, but none of it made any sense, none of it connected in any useful or helpful way. He latched all the tanks closed and looked down at his arm. It throbbed, it hurt and was turning dark with infection. It was likely the slime on the creature that had attacked him was toxic. But he didn't have any way to treat it. He was terrified he would look down and see the same red glow in his veins as they had seen in those victims and these animals. But so far, it was just a horrible scratch.

He wasn't well, they both knew it. He was clammy and sweaty, his stomach hurt. He offered Lisa a small smile before taking out his phone and dialing Morgan's number, hoping this would be the time they answered. But it went immediately to voicemail. Again. He wasn't ready to admit that the team they had worked with for months was probably dead, torn apart by monsters in a small South Texas town. He dialed Jordan's number, and when that was busy, he worked his way down the list, attempting to call every contact he had on the team. None of them answered, not that he had expected them to. He moved to the passenger side of the car and brushed off all the glass he could before sitting down. Now he felt guilty about making Lisa sit in the glass for so many hours.

"Lisa," he said as she was getting in. He waited for her to turn and look at him. "I'm sorry, for, for all of this. If I don't make it to San Antonio ..."

"Shut up, Freddy." She looked away from him, pulling the seatbelt on and adjusting the mirrors. "Just shut up. We're almost to San Antonio. We'll go straight to the police, get you to a hospital, and start finding answers. Okay?" She looked over at him and reached out to take his hand, giving it a squeeze. His skin was hot, burning up as though he were fighting off some infection.

"Okay." He didn't sound convinced. "Let's talk. Let's figure out some hypothesis while you drive, keep me distracted. First hypothesis, it's an alien parasite."

"I thought you would want to be serious,"

"I am serious! I'm at a loss, Lisa. What could do this? Any of this?" Ferdinand laughed at the absurdity of the situation. He was a scientist, a man dedicated to analyzing the evidence in front of him. The evidence in front of them, however, was inane.

"If the changes were happening between generations, we could look at what was causing an acceleration of the evolutionary process, but inside a single life span, I mean inside this car ride, something is causing rapid mutation." Lisa bit her lip, considering all of the possibilities. Radiation could cause birth defects that sometimes seemed like strange mutations, but this bordered on comic book science fiction.

"The only thing I can think of that causes change that quickly is tumors," Ferdinand offered, leaning back against the car seat and closing his eyes.

"What if it's a combination of things?" Lisa offered softly.

"A combination of things that is effecting human, aquatic, and amphibious life?"

"Yes! What do we know that mutates and evolves rapidly? Viruses and bacteria."

"You're suggesting this is a disease?" Ferdinand checked himself, there wasn't much use in being incredulous when they had a seven-eyed, five-footed salamander in the trunk.

"I'm suggesting there's something in the speed of the mutations that mimics the swift evolutionary changes we would normally associate with a virus."

They both sat silently for a few moments, their minds working over the various possibilities, how to connect the dots. Both of them were world class biologists, but neither of them was a geneticist. They knew enough to work in their fields. Ferdinand considered the idea of something causing these mutations from an evolutionary standpoint. That would need to be their first call once they got to a lab, someone who could figure out what was happening at a genetic level.

***

An axolotl crawled across the ground away from the burning wreckage of the van Jordan Mills had been driving. The research team had never made it past George West. The first car in their little caravan had been ambushed as they slowed down. The cars behind them fared no better as they came to a halt in order to avoid hitting the cars in front of them. It was a massacre as the vehicles were swarmed with what was once the populace of the small town. They had ripped the driver out of the first car and piled in the hole where the door had been. Claws and fangs and mandibles swung, tearing into the still human victims in the car. The rest of the town descended on the other cars, drawn in by the screams of fear.

Morgan kicked open the door, fleeing Vanessa's gurgled screams that were forcing themselves past her ruptured face. Morgan didn't look, she just ran. She could hear the strange strangled screams of the monsters as they tore into her friends. She stumbled and ran, refusing to look back even as the monsters howled for blood. She could hear the wet tearing as the research team was devoured, the tortured scream of metal being broken as the creatures frantically tore at the vehicles to get to the creamy meat filling. Her mind reacted violently against the sounds behind her, triggering her to flee without thought or concern for where she was going. There was nothing else but flight in her. Her pants stuck to her leg where she had pissed herself, but she didn't care, she only cared about running. As quickly and as far as she could. Away from the carnage, away from the monsters, away from everything that was happening.

Morgan hopped a fence into a pasture. Her side burned in protest at the strenuous physical activity, and she finally looked over her shoulder and realized she hadn't been chased beyond the town. She was alone. Collapsing where she stood, Morgan took in deep, gasping breaths. She was drenched in the gore of her friends, bits of flesh and bone stuck in her hair from when the things had begun tearing Vanessa apart. Morgan wept, curling into a ball against the terror her mind was screaming at her.

Her wailing was interrupted by a discordant moo. She looked up and screamed. She continued screaming until the thing that was once a cow tore out her lungs.

***

"Fred, wake up."

Ferdinand opened his eyes and then sat up in a shock, sweating. They were outside of San Antonio, just outside, and the city was burning. Smoke hung in the sky, obscuring the tops of the tallest buildings. In front of them, a military blockade had been set up. Lisa slowed the car as they approached the line of military vehicles and finally came to a stop as a soldier approached their SUV with a hand raised and a rifle pointed at them. Fred straightened in his seat as much as he was able. He spared a glance at his arm, still infected, still angry, but no signs of glowing veins or mutation. Maybe he was safe from becoming a monster, even if he did succumb to poison or infection, there were after all, fates worse than death.

Lisa rolled down the window and raised both hands, glancing at Ferdinand to get him to do the same. She didn't ask what was going on, she could guess. The mutations had reached San Antonio, which was terrifying in and of itself. How bad was it? How much of the population was infected?

"Sorry, folks, city is closed. Can't let anyone in."

"Sir, please, you have to let us get to—"

"Ma'am, all due respect, but I said ain't no one getting in right now. Habla ingles?" He asked glanced at Ferdinand.

"Si, yo hablo," Ferdinand responded, leaning over. "Pero, escuchen. Nosotros tenemos informacion para las policia o officiales de cuidad." He paused, watching the young soldier processing this bit of news. "We need to get to the people in charge. We were studying these mutations down on the border. We can help." It wasn't exactly true; Ferdinand had no idea if they could help or not. But they did probably know more than anyone else dealing with the issue.

The soldier stepped away, speaking into a radio at his shoulder. He seemed to be reporting in, and after a few moments, he approached the car again. "You think you can help?"

"We're scientists. We have information that may be pertinent to these developments," Lisa said, dropping her hands to the steering wheel.

"Okay, we're going to get you inside and get you an escort to the base." He mumbled something into his radio and then put a hand on the car door. "You've seen this in other places? They won't tell us anything. It's not just happening in San Antonio?"

He looked afraid, and Ferdinand understood that, of course he understood that after what they had seen. "No, we saw it in small towns. I'm sorry, we don't know how wide spread it is yet. But we know there are signs of mutation as far south as the Rio Grande. I have to assume further south than that."

The soldier stepped back from the car. He looked hopeless. The news that this was not an isolated event taking place in San Antonio but something sweeping through South Texas was devastating to him. He had family in the valley and in Mexico. He waved them forward wordlessly, his mind on what would happen to his mother.

As promised, two military vehicles, M-ATVs, pulled up in front of and behind them, with manned M60E4s swiveling to sweep the streets as they moved. It made Ferdinand's blood run cold. It spoke volumes to how dire the situation here actually was. The city was burning, but surely it wasn't as bad as they had seen in George West; there, the city had been crushed. San Antonio had police and military, monsters couldn't destroy the entire city ... he hoped.

His hopes swiftly began to dissolve as they drove into the city. Many areas seemed relatively untouched. Most, really. But as they passed by poorer sections of the city, that changed. That was where the brunt of the violence existed. The guns roared as they spat streams of lead at the once-human creatures that scurried between buildings. The creatures had apparently learned to fear the sound of gunshots, and they were relatively unbothered as they drove, the gunners keeping any of the more curious mutated away. Finally, after a grueling hour of weaving between abandoned cars, Lisa parked at a joint branch military base.

Glancing over at Ferdinand, she realized he was slipping further. She prayed they would have medical facilities on base. She unbuckled and got out, looking towards the approaching men, decked out in their uniforms. Neither they nor her had any idea of how truly terrible things were. She took a few steps towards them, gesturing back to the SUV.

"My colleague is hurt, and we have live specimens in the back of the vehicle. Do you have a lab I can set up in?" She had learned early in her career that the best way to deal with men in authoritative positions was to go on the offensive, start off by demanding the things you needed. The officers looked taken aback that this random citizen, a small Indian woman at that, had hopped out of the car and started listing off demands. But these men hadn't succeeded in the military by being easily flustered, or by ignoring orders. It was baked into their DNA. Immediately, one of the men, a sergeant from his uniform, spoke to an aide, who immediately ran off.

"Ma'am, I'm afria—" he began.

"Doctor. Doctor Chibuzo, and my colleague is Doctor Sila. He was poisoned when he shot one of the creatures. I also need a phone so I can contact another colleague, a geneticist. We think we can figure all of this out with those pieces." She stopped, realizing she was starting to sound less authoritative and more manic.

"Okay, Doctor," the man said once she had finished talking. He was a bit older, Hispanic, with sad drooping eyes. "Our lab equipment isn't fantastic. We can essentially provide the tools that our medical and forensic teams have access to, which isn't much." He nodded to the SUV behind Lisa, where a team of medics had suddenly appeared and were extracting Ferdinand. "Now, you've come in here saying you can help. How about we go sit down while they take care of your friend and you explain what's going on, how you can help, and maybe explain what the Abhorrent itself is." He saw her blank look. "The monster, we're calling it Abhorrent."

"Monster. You mean monsters." Abhorrent was certainly an accurate, if somewhat dehumanizing, term for the creatures that attacked them in George West, Lisa thought. But the general's face didn't look optimistic or agreeable with her assessment. "The mutated people," Lisa said, her voice cracking with the need for him to confirm that they were talking about the same thing, that there wasn't anything worse in the world than the mutated people. She felt a massive ball of fear rising in her chest.

"No, Doctor, I mean *the* monster."

**

What was unknown to Lisa Chibuzo, what was being explained to her, was that a massive *abhorrent* creature had been spotted west of San Antonio, emerging from

Medina Lake and approaching the city. Even as they spoke, the Air Force was sending jets to engage the target. They were scrambling other heavy ordinance, but as most of that was in Killeen, it was unlikely it would arrive in San Antonio before the monster did. Not to mention Killeen was suffering its own attacks of creatures. There, the creatures poured out of the RV parks, painting the countryside red.

The monster was pale blue except for the angry red glow of its veins beneath its skin. Pink, feathery fronds surrounded its head, quivering and wiggling in the wind as it took each earth-shaking step. From its mouth and from the large fronds, a thick red mist poured out with each laborious breath. Around it crawled the mutated and monstrous. A cohort of screaming tortured flesh and hunger, driven by instinct and fear to follow in their new god's footsteps. The ponderous creature hungered; it was driven not by the hunger, though, but by need. It knew that somewhere it would find a mate. Deep in its amphibious brain, it understood it could not stay put in the warm waters of the rivers it had grown in. That it would find no mate there, that food was too scarce there. As it moved, its massive head tilted, observing the creatures that skittered around it. They were everywhere, a howling circus of twisted monstrosities. They scurried and slithered, they galloped and flew around its head. These were its family in a way, but they were also food. The creature bent its neck and swept hundreds of the creatures into its maw before swinging its head up and crushing them to a pulp with its hard palate and swallowing. Fog bellowed out of its gills and mouth; it needed to stay wet. Emerging from the lake was a necessity because of the need for food and migration, but it was not ideal.

It saw silver and black birds approaching, predators. The birds were larger than any others it had seen, and they flew at it screaming, firing projectiles at it. The bullets hit the creature's rubbery skin, some even penetrated and caused glowing blood to leak from small wounds that quickly scabbed over and began healing. But these were pinpricks against its thick slick hide that did no real damage. It felt no pain from these, but it recognized that this was aggression, that the swift screaming birds were attacking it. It twisted its neck, watching as the birds flew away and then circled back. This time, the scream from the birds was almost unbearable as missiles streaked from their underbellies and exploded against the axolotl's face. The fire stung its eyes, it cracked the skin and caused pain, less from the actual missile and more from the evaporation of moisture.

It roared and reared up onto its hind legs, the sudden impossible movement so much faster than anything its size should be able to move. It swept forward again, knocking a plane out of the air. The bodies of its legion of mutated minions cushioned the colossal animal's fall back to the earth. But still the tremors were felt even in San Antonio. Undeterred, unslowed, and increasingly angry, the salamander god of the evolved marched towards the city.

John Baltisberger

Chapter 6

Barbara was frustrated. She had eaten plenty before the people had swarmed, but she had been forced to regurgitate her wonderful meal. Now she had a mostly safe place and a mate that couldn't leave her to go waste his semen in one those pretty dumb bimbos that Owen thought she didn't know about. Before, it had always been an ego thing. Why was he disrespecting her so much? Were they prettier? Was she too fat? What was wrong with her that made him want to go fuck some tramp? Now those thoughts seemed silly. She should have just found them and killed them. He had done it because she had *let* him. By not fighting the tramps and showing her dominance, she had allowed him to be a less than stellar mate.

Mate. What was left of Barbara's face twisted in rage at the thought. He hadn't even wanted to mate! How many times had he pulled away from finishing the job like a proper male and made her taste his weak and watery cum? She had done it because he seemed to like it, because that's what he wanted. Her new brain railed against wants, it focused on needs. Making

Owen happy was no longer a thing she cared about. It confused her and made her head hurt that she had ever wanted to please him. Now she would get what *she* wanted. She would get what she needed. She would call the shots, and Owen would do what he needed to do to prove himself a worthy mate; or he would prove to her and himself that he wasn't worth the meat that made up his less than impressive body.

As Barbara stalked the streets of the King William's district, she caught a whiff of something powerful, a near stench that would turn the stomach of any woman in her right mind. But Barbara's nose was different now. It parsed the stench of death and bile from the more subtle chemical signals behind it. Yes, it reeked in a way that made her aware she was in another's territory now. But it wasn't just someone else's territory. It was a male's territory. She could smell the masculinity under the reek of urine. The urine was fine, healthy, it would warn off other males. She immediately thought of her rescuer from earlier, he was strong and had waded in to fight her attackers easily. She drooled at the thought of the strong traits he could pass on. A part of her deep in her brain reminded her that sex could be fun and pleasureful, but that wasn't even secondary now, it wasn't even a concern that registered. She wanted fertile, she wanted strong.

She thought again of Owen and his watered-down, weak semen. What sort of weak runt bullshit young would he give her? Would they even survive in the eggs? Barbara licked her chin, allowing her two tongues to slide across her teeth and the scabbed-over remnants of her lips. There was a lust, a needy warmth that spread from between her thighs to her extremities. She didn't need weak, mewling Owen, she needed a real male. A real male with real spunk that would be deposited in her to fertilize her. Not wasted dribbling down her chin in a superficial display of pseudo-dominance. She decided she would find and make this male her own.

Barbara skittered through the shadows, following the reeking, fetid odor of urine and musk. The stench was everywhere. The male had taken time to carefully mark his territory. It was an intoxicating smell, the uric acid and ammonia mixing with the vomited bile of a male that was strong enough to eat more than his fill. These were the genes she wanted to gift to her offspring. She would have him. She gurgled with excitement and was rushing towards the doors of the building all the smells led to her when suddenly she froze, her blood running cold.

There was another female.

Another female was following the scent towards what Barbara had decided was her man. The female was a ponderous thing with seven legs and twitching grotesque arms sprouting from the rolls of fat that hung loosely between the spines of bone that had sprouted to support the weight of the obese woman's form. It wasn't a coincidence either. The female was splaying her body open, warbling for the male to come and take her. She nearly vibrated in the street, welcoming the male to his meal. Her folds of supple, soft fat flesh quivered with the movement, sending waves of stale sweat stink from within the chasms of her meat flaps. Barbara was disgusted. What this female wanted was *hers*. More than that, she would waste the good seed on her rotting weakness. They would die off because this woman wanted to pass on her piss-poor genetics. Barbara was a better choice.

Barbara let out a shrill scream and charged forward on three legs, her claws already swinging through air in a threatening display. The large female turned, her multiple chins wagging with the movement, flinging spittle and slimy pus through the air. Her cheeks peeled back, splaying her mouth open, revealing a lamprey-like circle of teeth that moved independently. Barbara normally hated confrontation, and she would never have taken on someone bigger than her like this before her molt into her current form. But now she was powerful. She would not be denied by this mound of sagging lard.

At the last moment, Barbara leapt, bringing her third leg up in a vicious kick, using the sharp bony claws that had grown at discordant angles on her foot to slash at the other female. The flesh was leathery and tough, and there was more resistance than she expected, but still she was able to tear into the meat. Yellow cottage cheese textured fat spilled out of the cut, and the female roared in challenge and pain. She folded over her own fat, squeezing out more of the fat like a lumpy, wretched tube of toothpaste, trying to protect herself from Barbara's assault. Barbara didn't relent, clawing and biting at the exposed flesh, aiming for eyes, nipples, and anything that looked softer.

The female screamed in frustration and surged forward, carrying Barbara with her. Several arms wrapped around, grabbing and pulling at Barbara. Despite the flabby appearance, the sheer mass of the other female was more than capable of pulling Barbara off and flinging her against the nearby wall. Barbara squealed in pain, dazed by the impact, but the waddling approach of the larger female was slow enough that Barbara had time to get back to her feet and dodge the incoming flurry of blows from the blobbish rival. Barbara sunk low and scuttled under the other female as quickly as she was able, hoping to get behind her. The other woman seemed to sense it and dropped suddenly, putting all of her considerable weight down and crushing Barbara's third leg under her.

Barbara howled in pain and frustration. She was trapped. Panic filled her mind, but there was still a part of her that could think rationally, a part of her that knew she could still win and get the man who would pump her full of life-giving sperm. She twisted, ignoring the pain, and attacked the backside of the woman with her mangled teeth, tusks, and claws. The flesh was tough here too, but softer than the front. Barbara tore into the woman, ripping out deep, quivering hunks of flesh as she went. Burying her face in the woman's bulk, her two tongues latched inside the woman's anus, the hooks on the surface ripping up the soft flesh and pulling Barbara's head forward, inside the larger female. She snapped and bit, scrabbling for purchase, her tongues shooting out to re-latch and pull the woman's intestines out of her rectum through sheer force. Barbara felt the flesh give way and felt the hardness of bone against her face. She pulled her tongues back in, ignoring the taste of decaying old feces, and opened her mouth as wide as the tight tunnel of the woman's ass would allow and chomped down on her rival's tailbone.

She couldn't hear the panicked screams and screeches from her rival, and she wouldn't have felt mercy or sympathy if she could. Barbara continued to chew and rip her way up and through the body of the larger female until she felt the fresh air on her hand. Swimming forward in a sea of fat, gristle, and bone, Barbara pushed her way out of the stomach of the corpse. Gore and viscera dripped from every inch of her body. Though her third leg hung uselessly now, she had killed her rival, she would claim the prize, and indeed, the struggle and combat had attracted the attention of the male in the building, who was now pushing through the doors of the apartment building.

Barbara was shocked to see Carl Northrup there. Somewhere in the back of her brain, the few neurons that were Barbara fired in revulsion at the thought of seeing not only the junkie old man, but that she had just killed a woman, eaten her way through the woman's asshole to fuck this man. But he wasn't the same Carl Northrup she had turned away from the methadone clinic this morning. He was bigger, stronger, he reeked of masculine musk and piss and power. He was the male she was looking for. His misshapen torso convulsed with extra musculature. And between his legs, three cocks twisted and writhed, hardening with arousal, and his scrotum was swelling and rippling at the promise of procreation.

Barbara licked her lips, where her lips used to be. She didn't care who it was, she especially didn't care who he had been before who he was now. He was a virile and promising male. Barbara turned her back towards him and bent over, letting her ass splay and displaying the swollen folds of her labia in welcome. It was crusted with cysts from ingrown hairs that had been caught in the swell of mutation, and bits of bone now pushed through, spreading her for an easier if somewhat punishing entry. But they couldn't mate here. As much as she wanted to feel all three of those bumpy crusted rods thrusting into her, she wanted to do this somewhere safe, somewhere she wouldn't risk having to fight more females.

She scuttled forward as he approached, leading him on, forcing him to chase. Carl jabbered in frustration and let out several hoots of discordant noise in protest, but he followed. In his own mind, he knew this was that little cock tease of a nurse from the clinic. But beyond that, he knew she was a strong female, and from the smell of her vaginal secretions hitting his malformed nose, she was ready and ripe for insemination. This was the thing he needed. He needed to deposit his genetic information in this female and ensure that the strong survived and the weak died. The weak like his sister, who now lay dead and torn apart by the creature leading him to her den with her displayed sex.

***

Mike waited until nearly nightfall. He considered trying to steal a car in the parking garage in order to throw the police off his trail, but he had to admit to himself he had no idea how to hotwire anything. Mike had lived his life trying to be a good person but had always thought that when the chips were down, he would outperform most other men. He was an Eagle Scout, he watched shows like *Survivor* and read books on survival. Now sitting in a parking garage with a scared seven-year-old with a bug out bag and camping equipment, Mike realized he had no real skills for survival. Once they got to the campground, what would they do for food? What would they do once the battery on Abby's tablet ran out? Mike rested his head against the steering wheel, trying to parse out what he could possibly do to salvage anything resembling a life. He wasn't some action hero who could survive the world after it blew up.

"Daddy?"

"Yeah, honey?" Mike answered without lifting his head.

"I'm done playing."

Mike nodded; she was bored. "Well it's almost bedtime, honey. Why don't you try to get some sleep? I'll wake you up when we get to the campsite." He started the car, immediately relishing the cool movement of air from the air conditioner. He felt bad, not just guilty or scared, but physically bad. He glanced down at his side; his shirt was sticking to his side as blood oozed out. Every time he moved, it felt like he was ripping the scab open and pouring salt in the wound. He could feel the slow pulse of pain that radiated from his side. For the first time, he considered going to the hospital. He could get treated. Maybe he could claim his car was stolen if the police were looking for him. But if he didn't get this treated, would he even be able to survive?

He sat there, hands on his steering wheel, considering the two options. Hospital or Cibolo Gardens campground? He had done the most basic first aid, but he probably needed stitches, he needed antibiotics. Mike let out a long suffering sigh and pulled out of the parking garage and began backtracking through the edge of the city towards Northeast Baptist Hospital. It was closer to central San Antonio than he wanted to be, but it was the closest to where he was.

The streets were filled with fear and smoke. The hours that had passed hadn't made things any calmer. Instead, the violence and fear seemed to have ramped up. The positive was the cops must have been too busy to deal with Mike—when monsters roamed the streets, the human monsters were allowed free passage. He kept his handgun in his lap again, less for the police and more in case any monsters approached. Human or otherwise. He realized he hadn't even thought about the cop he had killed outside of his own fear of going to jail. He had murdered two people and didn't even feel guilty. He could tell himself it was because he would do literally anything to protect Abby, but it scared him.

That cop had had family, parents, maybe a wife and kids ... now there would be a hole in their lives where he had once been. And Mike didn't care. He had always told himself he was an empathetic person. His hand twitched on the gun in his hand; he felt like his paranoia was growing. People and monsters, monsters and people. Was there any difference? They could both be dangerous. The police would surely have pulled him away from his daughter. He couldn't allow that, he had to protect his young. He had to shelter her, to feed her.

Mike shook his head, trying to clear it of the sudden haze and anger he felt in that moment. His stomach lurched. He had fed his young, but he hadn't eaten yet. His own feeding had been interrupted by a rival. No, not a rival. Laura. Laura had attacked him and Abby. He took a long deep breath, turning off of the main road to enter the hospital parking lot, and hit the brakes. The hospital was burning, more than burning, he could see the creatures climbing out of windows and over it. An entire swarm of the inhuman monsters, they had claimed this place. It would be a place of spawning and violence, a feast of meat and offal. His stomach lurched again. Mike glanced in the mirror to look back at Abby; she was asleep. That was good. She didn't need to see all of this.

He put the car in reverse and left the hospital to its swarming chaos. He would head north like he originally planned, find a good place in the Cibolo Gardens area to set up his nest. No, his tent. Mike shook his head again. Something was wrong with his thoughts, but he couldn't quite place it, something was interfering. It could be the pain, or perhaps just emotional and physical exhaustion from trying to run and deal with the guilt of killing his wife. The guilt he had shoved down so far into a dark hole of his heart that he couldn't even see it. Was he in shock? His side still hurt, but not as much as he would have thought it should. And he was emotionally deadened. Did shock do that? Mike grasped the steering wheel with both hands, taking his hand off the gun for a moment, realizing how cramped his hand had gotten just gripping the gun for so long.

He looked back at Abby again. He felt the flood of

love and relief that she was okay. No, he wasn't in shock, he wasn't a sociopath incapable of empathy. Laura had killed herself and their marriage with the pills. The cop would have hurt Abby. Mike had done the right thing, and there was nothing that could convince him he hadn't done the right thing in protecting his little girl. He turned back towards the road. He would always protect her; he would keep her safe through this crisis far away from the frantic bustle of monsters and the swarming danger of people.

John Baltisberger

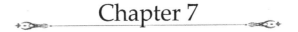

Chapter 7

Lisa Chibuzo sat in a room by herself, watching the static filled screen of a TV. The video footage of the monster had finished playing minutes ago, but she was unable to bring herself to move. She remembered the massive gouges next to the river near George West. This thing had come from the Rio Grande; it was the end product of the mutations and evolutions they had seen in the specimen just a day ago. She recognized the thing as an axolotl, or rather, it had been one at some point. But that seemed impossible. How could such a creature exist? From the video and smattering of reports and data gathered, the monster was beyond colossal, at least 30 meters tall and over 100 meters long from her estimation, though it could easily be larger. But how?

How could something that large exist? How could it have grown in the Rio Grande, which even at its deepest point was only roughly 20 meters deep? How large could it have grown in those waters before the environment became unsustainable and it had to seek more food and a larger body of water? Could it survive in brackish waters? Or even salt water? Was it merely using the surface waterways of Texas to maneuver around, or had it gotten into the aquafers, caves, and watersheds of the state? And perhaps least pressingly, was it the source of the mutations they had been seeing in the specimens or a byproduct of them itself? From the screaming and the hurried reports during the video, more of the mutated monsters—the afflicted, as they were being called by the soldiers—were swarming around the monster. If it was the source of the changes and it had gotten into the ground water of Texas, was the entire state now poisoned, spreading mutation far and wide? And what about the mist they described as a red fog pouring from the gills of the creature? Though, the poor-quality video had made that impossible to see for herself.

In the silence of the room, Lisa distracted herself from the fear of the unknown by wondering why it was that for all the advancements in video equipment and small portable cameras, the footage looked like someone recorded it with an old 8mm hand crank camera. The grainy image hid too many details. She needed a clear image if she was to really make any sort of scientific jabs at discerning what was happening. When she first arrived on base, she had fired off several emails and even sent faxes to several colleagues, people whose expertise might have some possibility of cracking the code of what was happening in Texas. She felt small and helpless in a way she hadn't felt since leaving Kolkata, leaving behind the stifling patriarchy of her home. She was about to rewind and replay the video when a couple of the base staff, a medic and a forensic scientist, walked in, interrupting her reflection.

"Dr. Chibuzo?"

"Yes." She had lost a lot of the steam she had when she first came onto base. She was scared, and so, so tired. Sitting in this chilly room watching footage of something that could not possibly exist but most certainly did had destroyed the last of her hope. She shook her head, trying to clear away the fatalism. "How is Freddy?"

The two looked at each other, their mouths in grim lines.

"He's unresponsive right now."

"When we got him into the bed, he passed out, and we haven't been able to wake him up." The medic's name tag identified her as Sergeant Ranalli, and Lisa wondered what sort of medical certification came with that.

Lisa rose, eager to check on her friend herself, but the medic put up a hand.

"Our team is looking after him. We need you here finding a solution," Ranalli said quickly.

"A solution?" Lisa stammered. "I'm not a toxicologist. We need someone who can—"

"Not for your friend, for the creatures," the scientist whose badge identified him as a Lieutenant Lawhon said, then he paused, seeing her frustration. "We need to figure out how to kill it."

Lisa threw her hands in the air in exasperation. "I am a scientist, not a killer. You have drones and bombs and missiles and guns. Just kill it."

"Nothing we've thrown at it has gotten through," the scientist, if Lisa could call him that, answered. Before Lisa could respond, he held up a laptop. "Your colleagues are ready to go over the notes you sent them."

Lisa was about to retort that they shouldn't need a team of world-renowned scientists on hand to figure out how to kill a thing. She had hoped they could save people, that whatever they had discovered in the Rio Grande might have the answers to stopping the affliction that was changing people into ... whatever it was changing them into. But maybe she did need to consider why their weapons weren't working. If the massive siren wasn't stopped, there wouldn't be people to save. She remembered the toppled town of George West, ruined structures. The truth was that if the salamander was the gravest threat, the people that had mutated had to be connected to this monster somehow. She nodded and took the laptop, moving back to her seat.

Opening the laptop, she saw that the video conferencing program was already up and running. She gathered her notes in a little pile and tried to calm herself before hitting the call button and sitting in on the strangest and most important discussion of her life.

***

Just northeast of San Antonio, the gargantuan axolotl, the monster they called Abhorrent, was frustrated by the minuscule size of the water ways presented to it and feeling the mucus slime on its skin beginning to dry. Instinctively, the salamander understood that the mucus was what kept it safe, allowing it to breathe, to survive the sun. It had stopped the attacks of the tanks and aircraft that had fired on him. The salamander dug furiously into the ground, claws the size of city busses scrabbling at the bud and soft dirt as it pulled its body down. Animals and loping mockeries of humanity were crushed or cleaved with each motion, glowing blood soaking into the ground or joining the rush of water into the great gouges the god was carving into the tortured flesh of Texas.

Down into the Medina watershed, into the caves that crisscrossed under the great state, the abhorrent siren and its coterie of misshapen worshipers submerged themselves. Swimming, clawing, eating their way through the muck of the Lone Star State, unbeknown to them, they dug under the line of defenses, self preservation fueling a need for hydration and leading to avoiding the worst of the city's defenders. The military had seen the creature submerge but had no way to safely track its movements other than the tremors and the protestation of the earth beneath their feet. The soldiers scrambled to try to plan some way to combat this now unseen enemy.

The citizens of San Antonio were completely ignorant of what was happening, the shaking earth and crumbling buildings around them lost in the collateral damage of the monstrous attack of the afflicted. Pipes bursting and buildings collapsing was only a backdrop to the mutated masses of flesh and bone hunting not only the healthy but each other. Brawls broke out as the afflicted met and fought over territory, and when they had finished slaughtering one another, they sought food to replenish their energy. Beyond the monstrous afflicted, there were riots. The fearful and the angry, the opportunists and the greedy all swarmed, attempting to take advantage of the chaos, not realizing that every minute spent within the bounds of the city was another minute that death approached.

Until it exploded out from under Woodlawn Lake park.

Cement, water, and metal debris showered down on the city as Abhorrent smashed through the underside of the city to fresh air. Clouds of billowing red fog spread out like the fallout of a massive explosion, warping everything that breathed in the foul exhalations of the axolotl. Under the cruel ministrations of the mist, bones bent even as they grew sharp protrusions. Flesh buckled and warped, splitting under the pressure from expanding muscles and new organs that grew out of a forced bonding of the DNA that was so alien and hostile to their bodies.

Worse still were the flocks of things that had been birds before Abhorrent's unkind embrace had afflicted them, gifting them with new forms more pleasing to the new God of the earth. They flew into the red tinged San Antonio night and searched for food. Buzzards with too many eyes and chitin pincers for claws snapped at humans as they ran for cover. They dove down and burrowed into the flesh of the humans, only to be devoured themselves within minutes when some larger afflicted terrestrial found the buffet of meat on display in the streets. Feral and family pets were quick to change, their small lungs stiffening into bronchial moss to deliver the morphing mutagenic organic gas throughout their bodies. Cats with more legs than lives scurried across ceilings to get into the cribs of small and delicious infants that popped and cracked in their newly segmented mouths.

What few households held no afflicted were soon broken into by ravenous creatures looking for an easy meal of the soft and fleshy unafflicted. As the hours stretched on, the afflicted seemed more and more capable in hunting down their human prey. Chitinous scabby plates grew over flesh to protect them from bullets. Their horrid screams echoed across the city to one another, coordinating attacks on places the humans dug in.

In the shadow of their god, the afflicted swarmed over the population, only stopping long enough to devour the offal leavings of the dead.

***

Lisa was pulling out her hair in frustration. On the laptop screen, her fellow scientists were doing the same, though likely for different reasons. They were watching the devastation of San Antonio on TV monitors, on the news, on TikTok, videos of people who would be dead within minutes of uploading the video. They saw and understood what was happening as well as any of them could. But the other scientists weren't *in* San Antonio, they weren't here where it was happening. They couldn't feel the ground trembling under their feet, they couldn't feel the deep thrum caused by the emergency sirens that was causing her fillings to ache.

"I understand that you took these images yesterday, Lisa," Dr. Gwendyln Stevens said for likely the seventh time. Even the two soldiers with her rolled their eyes as Stevens continued to make excuses.

The other scientist on the call, Karl Dovijc, was tapping his fingers on the desk, clearly agitated in front of the camera.

"What Stevens is trying to say is that genetics don't work the way you are trying to make them work. Nothing works this way." Karl's voice could sneer while he was smiling. He was a greasy asshole known for trying to sleep with any woman in a lab coat who happened to be at a conference. He had been moved between universities for scandals with students more times than anyone could count. But he was one of the best.

"Same species, from the same area, taken at the same time; the only difference is the time of death!" Lisa snapped.

"Then they aren't the same species, Lisa."

"Doctor Chibuzo!" Lisa snapped, unwilling to let Karl think that his slimy shit eating grin was disarming to her in anyway. She could see the smirk on his mouth and she wished she could wipe it off.

"But the samples, you see the paperwork just the same as I do. This is CRISPR DNA in an animal where it should not be present! You can't tell me that these fragments designed to alter DNA aren't in some way responsible for the changes we're seeing!"
" I can, and I am!" Stevens snapped. "My god, Chibuzo,

I understand you're a top expert in your field, but in this case, you don't know what the hell you are talking about. I am telling you definitively, that even if this is CRISPR DNA sequences—"

"It is," Lisa interrupted.

"*Even if it is*," Stevens emphasized, "it wouldn't cause the sort of mutations you are seeing. There's another explanation."

Lisa buried her face in her arms on the desk and reached with one hand to close the laptop, ending the call. These were worthless, unhelpful, and stubborn. She wished they would posit a theory, any theory, rather than just shooting down her ideas. She felt a hand on her shoulder. Glancing up, she smiled sadly at the medic.

"Sorry, Sergeant, I'm just very tired."

"You can call me Gina, but, maybe instead of trying to figure out how this happened, we should focus on how to stop it." She glanced up at the scientist. "Right, Aaron?"

He jumped at his name being used, his attention brought back to the present.

"I think that would be smart."

Lisa nodded and reopened the laptop. Pulling open her email, she found the contacts she needed and started sending out invites again to attempt to get more *qualified* scientists into her brain trust to deliver a solution to the Abhorrent crisis.

***

Further south, Mike drove into the park unmolested. It worried him that there was no one at the gate, no one stopping him from just driving in. He watched the trees and the road carefully, not trusting his eyes. In the backseat, Abby was still asleep, the fear and freaking out over when he shot the cop had her exhausted. As far as he could tell, she hadn't connected the dots between the gunshot when he killed the cop and the shots that had killed her mother. He would have to confess that Mommy wasn't joining them eventually, he would have to explain to her that he had killed her mother to save her. He drove on, his own body exhausted by the ordeals of the day. The pain was back too. He wished he had brought Laura's painkillers with them, but all he had was their first aid kit.

He paused at the empty ranger's station and grabbed a site map. It was eerie. There were no signs of any attacks here, no sprays of blood or diseased creatures, just an empty station and gift shop. Mike grabbed a duffel bag off the shelf and shoved bottles of water, snacks, and other camping supplies into the bag. He had a lot of these supplies already, but having more wouldn't be a bad thing. Once he was stocked up, he checked the back office, and just as he hoped, a rifle was laying against the wall. He grabbed it and spent a few moments going through drawers to squirrel away any extra ammo. When he heard the car door outside, he realized he had left Abby alone with diseased monsters prowling the world. His heart frozen and his throat tightened to the point of choking in fear, Mike ran back out, finding Abby just playing with the door.

"Damnit, Abby! You scared me!" He grabbed her door and slammed it shut, wincing as the sound echoed across the forested area. He was about to shout something, just to vent his frustration, but realized that yelling would be just as damning in giving away their position as the slammed door. And besides, Abby was crying in the back seat now. He had scared her.

Armed and supplied, Mike got back in the car, tossing his haul in the passenger seat. He sat in silence, his heart still pounding and the world spinning from the sudden anxiety her door had given him. He listened to Abby sniffling in the back seat. She was trying to hold back her tears, trying to be a big girl.

"I'm sorry, honey, I just had to grab some supplies. When I heard the door, I thought someone was trying to grab you. I shouldn't have yelled, I'm sorry," he repeated. He watched her in the mirror as she sniffled and refused to look at him. Guilt welled up in his chest. He had killed her mother, and now he was yelling at her and slamming doors in her face. He had to be the worst father in the world. "We're gonna drive down the way a little bit and then set up camp, okay?"

"Do I have to sleep in my own tent?" Abby asked after several minutes of silence.

She was scared of being alone in her own tent, and while he had brought it, Mike realized he didn't want her sleeping away from him. It was too scary. He was scared, and her being out of sight would be terrifying. When he had bought the tents, the last time they went camping, Mike had been trying to bring the romance back into the marriage. Now, without Laura around, it didn't make sense to force Abby to sleep in her own tent alone.

"No, you can sleep in the tent with Daddy," he answered, smiling with as much kindness as he could muster at her. It would let him watch over her. If anything came into the tent, he would be there, gun ready to blast it to kingdom come.

"Okay! Can I watch my ponies until I go to sleep?"

"Honey, maybe we can find something else."

"But I like ponies!"

"I know you do, but you've watched all of the episodes."

"I know, I restarted it!" she said happily.

Of course she did. She had watched and re-watched the entire series of that damn show more times than he could count. But she had just stopped crying, and he needed the peace.

"Yeah, okay, honey, you can watch your cartoons until you fall asleep, but we have to set up the tents first, okay?"

They passed several campsites on their way, each empty with no signs of life and a few signs of struggle. It seemed likely that people had changed into monsters out here too, but without food, they must have gone searching into the town. If that was true, then he should be safe here, this place would be abandoned.

Chapter 8

Owen had passed out hanging against the wall. For hours, he had struggled, bucking against the netting of dried mucus and bile that held him tight. He had stopped screaming the first time he saw something inhuman pass by the door. Finally, he had succumbed to exhaustion. But it was a light and fitful sleep, disturbed every time a noise intruded on the apartment or a shadow of some *thing* with jutting horns and sagging mottled skin passed by the door. He woke again as he heard the sounds of something scraping across the floor. Opening an eye, he was horrified to see the thing that had been Barbara had returned. She walked on her all fours, or rather all six, leading a behemoth of twisted, tortured flesh behind her. Owen could barely tell that the thing following her had once been a man.

His legs bent backwards and ended in saggy elephant like sacks of skin that wobbled as he walked. His torso was thick as a tree trunk and writhed like a wall covered in roaches. His head was sunken between two shoulders that had become swollen with weeping wounds around shards of bone that had punctured outward and then grown entwined, locking them in position. From his side, several more smaller pairs of arms dangled uselessly. But Owen was distracted by other things that were dangling.

Between the behemoth's legs hung three unmistakably cock shaped appendages. They wept a clear slime and twitched sporadically. Occasionally, the cock-tendrils would lurch forward, as if trying to capture Barbara. They would stay pointing and rigid for a moment before vomiting a foul gummy precum onto the floor and flopping back down. The smell was rancid. Barbara herself smelled like a budget Vegas whorehouse on the hottest day of summer while the septic tank was being cleaned. The smell of rancid cloying smegma and old stale cum turned Owen's stomach, and he vomited, coating the front of his netting it yet another layer of his own stomach acid. He realized at least part of the smell of shit and piss was coming from himself, but the smell that followed his girlfriend and the three-cocked thing was far worse than anything he had ever encountered before.

***

Barbara saw Owen, saw his revulsion and fear, and part of her was happy. He was afraid she was going to let some other male mount her. And she was. She opened an eye near the back of her head, and it rolled lazily before focusing first on Carl's strong upper body and then the plethora of rods below. The warmth of need and want spread through her. She realized somewhere within her misfiring brain that coming here hadn't just been about the safety of fucking in her nest but also about doing so in front of Owen, about repaying the

115

pain and humiliation he had visited on her. She wanted him to be part of this. She crawled forward, wiggling her ass back and forth, letting her vaginal fluids drip down her thighs and pool at her feet. She lifted off the ground, pressing her body against the netting holding Owen. She remembered when it mattered to her that she be petite and firm. Now her body was harder than ever, hardened into armor; it was a shell to protect her against predators and other females.

"Ohn," she murmured, a twitched, segmented finger stoking his jaw before she was ripped back and away from Owen.

Carl gripped her hips, and his cocks flailed wildly, each seeking entry independently. The sheath of chitin protecting his scrotum released, and the ponderous genitalia swung free as the first shaft found entry and pushed into Barbara. Almost like a hive mind, the other two cocks writhed around each other and punctured into Barbara's dripping and hungry gaping hole. As soon as he was in and he pressed into her, the spines on her labia closed like a trap, puncturing the penetrating organs and pelvis, holding him close, leaving only enough room to thrust into her harder and with more momentum with every juddering shove.

Barbara moaned, several of her eyes rolling back in her head. She would never have imagined having more than one cock inside her at once before today. She could never have imagined how full she would feel. Three eyes snapped back into focus on Owen's face, inches away from her own, as she took the brunt of Carl's rough and rapid fucking. She played it up a bit, her tongues lolling out like the faces of the girls in the comic books Owen was always looking at when he thought no one could see him. Her third arm came up and roughly scraped at her hardened nipples. She broke through the scabrous growths covered her breasts, letting the sour pus leak freely. She lapped it up, lost in the moment of euphoria from the feeling of Carl meeting her need in a way Owen had always refused to. She would be fertilized and would carry life, and the feeling of Carl's three massive penises inside her made her realize just how much she had settled on with Owen.

But still, somewhere where the last couple of synapses that were still Barbara were firing, *she loved him.* She felt guilty, not guilty enough to stop, but she didn't want him to feel like she didn't care for him. Even as she rocked back and forth with every frenzied howling plunge, she tore at the netting holding Owen in place. She peeled back her own dried, hardened vomit to free his loins. He was soiled, but the reek of his waste trapped by his pants was intoxicating in a way that she loved. She would happily lick him clean; he would *love* that. She tore at his jeans, leaving great bloody scratches down his legs. But she freed his meager member. It hung limply and close to his body, his testicles retracted to protect the boys. Tentatively, she wrapped a tongue around the shaft of his flaccid penis and the other ran its bumpy surface over his scrotum.

He recoiled in fear.

Hurt by his rejection, she surged forward, ripping into Owen with her teeth. He didn't want her? Fine! The broken shards of bone that made up her mouth tore into him easily. She snapped her mouth closed and pulled back, shredding his manhood. His genitals hung like wet and ragged newspaper. Owen started screaming again, and in response, Carl began trying to tear himself free of Barbara's grasp. Blood, red and glowing, poured from between the two lovers. Barbara needed him, or more correctly, she needed him to finish his job and inseminate her. She spat out the rest of Owen's tattered meat, still unwilling to swallow, and turned, her spine bending in impossible ways. Bits of chitin and scabs fell from her body as she turned almost 180 degrees to bite into Carl's throat.

His own eyes widened in shock, unsure how to respond. He could smell the person's blood and the female's sex. He could feel his own balls contracting and relaxing as he ejaculated with all three of his cocks.

So wrapped up in the feelings of orgasm and orgasmic hunger, for a moment he was oblivious to the female tearing into his throat and chest with claws and teeth. When he finally realized what was happening, he panicked, lifting Barbara off the floor and charging forward to slam her into the wall in an attempt to dislodge her.

Barbara, who hours before had burrowed into another female in an attempt to win this male, would not be dissuaded so easily.

Already, Carl was weakening. His next slam into the wall was more of a slump. Barbara didn't relent, peeling huge slabs of meat off his chest and swallowing them greedily. One last dig to Owen, she would rather have any other male in her mouth than him. She was no longer angry, though. Now she was spent. The fight with the fat female, leading Carl across the city on her hands and knees, her offering up in his face, and then the pounding she had just taken was exhausting. She needed to eat.

She could hear in the distance something massive was moving. A predator.

***

Barbara greedily ate as much of Carl as she could from his still twitching corpse, marveling that she had ever feared him. She took special care to dig into his brain pan and get at the delicious gray meat, her favorite treat. Owen had passed out. She knew she had to leave her nest, her den. Before the predator got too close, she would flee north. But she was loathe to leave Owen here. She would need him, need him to feed her young when they hatched. She skittered towards him to cut him down.

***

Barbara had held Owen close to her body as she fled the oncoming super predator. She was angry. The male she had loved was worthless and even now slowing her down. The male she had enlisted to impregnate her had been decent, but in the end, he was just like any other male … food. Barbara didn't know how long she ran, but she was aware that she was growing exhausted. She could no longer hear the screams and cries of her those like her. The ground no longer shook. She could hear water nearby; she knew that was perfect. She would need to dig a burrow where she could bury Owen once he was filled with her eggs. She would be able to store food there and hide from predators.

She stalked past the sign that said Cibolo State Park and down the path. The well-worn paths made her nervous, predators would use well-worn paths, and while she was sure in her ability to fight off most challengers, she had precious cargo. She continued on her path before catching the smell of meat. Not meat, male. It was faint and weak. She would need to replenish her strength again; she would need to pace herself better. She would need to lay her eggs inside Owen and then protect the eggs, not something she would be able to do if she was starving or running herself ragged.

She heard them, she heard the sound of many voices, and she almost panicked. How many of them were there? As she peered past the foliage she hid in, her mandibles worked in thought. Two. There were more voices than that, but they came from the little box the smaller one held. Girl. It was a little girl. Barbara sneered, another young thing that would compete for food, but there was a big male too. She let Owen fall to the ground. She would subdue these food items and then return to her incubator. She approached in silence, suppressing the urge to scream her challenge. She had to change, to evolve into an ambush predator for the good of her babies.

With a swift motion, she grabbed Abby and vomited hardening mucus over her face, silencing her before tossing her with cruel strength into a tree. From the resounding crack of her body, Barbara was confident the tiny human wouldn't get back up. With that, she moved on to the large male. She tackled him, already vomiting on him, the acid of her stomach acid burning him before the snotty phlegm began hardening. Mike couldn't break free of the mess of limbs that held him down.

Both subdued.

Barbara now let out a shrill scream of victory. She was the alpha predator. She would make this place her territory, her home. She would hunt here and feast on the flesh it offered. But first ...

She started to dig a new burrow, a place to store the meat she had already captured.

Chapter 9

Lisa was busily talking with other marine biologists and herpetologists. Now that she was no longer trying to figure out the why this crisis was on them, it was an easier time. They were capable of examining the evidence and positing hypotheses of how to counteract the monster they were faced with. It was clear that Abhorrent's mucus was protecting it against the weapons being thrown against it more than any natural armor. Just like in nature, the salamander was protected by a thick layer of slime that diffused the impact of any weapon and seemed to protect it from explosions as well. From the reports from the soldiers, the smaller mutated animals, it wasn't just humans, were evolving as the day went on.

They were evolving things like chitin plates and their own mucus membrane, making them harder to kill with the weapons they had on hand. But they could still be killed if enough firepower was brought against one of them. In the end, they all agreed this should be faced with fire, literal fire. A high enough concentration of heat and flames would cook and dehydrate any of the afflicted, and if applied in enough quantity, could even destroy the protective slime layer of the axolotl. In theory.

Lisa thanked everyone and slowly closed the laptop, ending calls for the second time tonight.

The solution was an airdrop of napalm. She didn't know much about military tactics or law, but it seemed like a huge amount of highly flammable ooze wouldn't be the most difficult thing to secure, and even if it were, the manufacture of napalm was easy. Use crop dusters to air drop a few thousand gallons of napalm on Abhorrent and cook the goddamn thing alive. It seemed like the easiest and most sensible solution.

"Okay." She rose with a stretch, realizing she had been cooped up in the small frigid lab for hours. "Now, that we have a plan, can I visit Freddy?" she asked, though she had no intention of letting them say no to her.

As if sensing her obstinate plans, Gina nodded with a sigh. "I don't see why not. We'll pop in on him on our way to see the general. You still have to pass on the plan."

"That is fine, so long as we see Freddy first."

Aaron stepped aside, letting Gina open the door and lead them out of the small room. They walked together down the hall. Lisa let the two lead her since she didn't know where anything was. She watched them use their badges on doors to scan through, disappointed. After a lifetime of watching dumb action movies and soldier movies with boyfriends and her brothers, she was expecting state of the art security. But from the looks of things, anyone with a free afternoon could be a spy on this base.

"So, Freddy ... are you guys a couple?" Aaron asked, his voice clearly indicating more than a passing interest.

From Gina's rolled eyes, Lisa could guess that this wasn't the first time she had been forced to put up with Aaron's lackluster flirting. She considered all the various answers to that question. They were friends, good friends, and she couldn't deny there was a certain ... chemistry between them. But Freddy had never moved on it, which wasn't surprising, she supposed, he was self-conscious. The scar that made him *El Guapo* also made him *El Inseguro*. But the truth was, she didn't want to answer any more of Aaron's questions.

"Yes. A couple. We met through work and things just worked out," she lied.

"Oh, well you know what they say."

"Aaron ..." Gina warned.

"What do they say?" Lisa asked.

"Never get your honey where you make your money!" he exploded triumphantly.

Gina rolled her eyes, but stifled a chuckle. Lisa laughed at the sentiment; it wasn't one she disagreed with. They were still chuckling at Aaron's outburst and rounding a corner when the sound of gunfire filled the air.

Lisa let out a frightened yelp, pressing against a wall.

Aaron looked back at her and grabbed her hand. "Stay with us!" he ordered.

Lisa was too frightened to argue, allowing him to pull her along the passageways until they burst out into the open air.

Outside, the scream of the sirens was deafening. It heightened her panic and fear, doing nothing to reassure her that things were under control. She took several steps past her escort, in awe of the sight of the guards and soldiers laying down fire against a tide of glowing red, mutated afflicted. In the distance she could see the massive bio-luminescent shape of Abhorrent stalking through the city, heedless of the destruction it caused.

The sirens were echoing across the world so loudly that Lisa didn't realize some of the screaming and gunfire was happening behind her. She turned in time to see an afflicted tearing into Gina. Lisa fell back in fear. Aaron lay on the ground, noisily sucking air through the hole in his chest. Bug-eyed, he stared at Lisa in disbelief and fear.

The afflicted had Gina by the throat. The spins on its rippling arm bristled, and it lunged forward, using its tongue to scoop out her eye and pop it beneath teeth that were being pushed out by new growth of bones. The creature's face was stretched by the mutations ripping their way through his body, the skull distending, forcing horns and splitting the jaw into three disparate parts to allow the afflicted to eat his prey whole if needed.

Abhorrent Siren

Despite all of the changes wrought on the tapestry of his flesh, the scar across Ferdinand's face made him easy to identify.

Lisa scrambled forward, praying Freddy's attention stayed on the woman he was mutilating. And he was; his claws, new bony protrusions growing from his fingers, were doing the work of careful surgery she had admired just a day ago as he cut open Gina's vest and bared her torso. He pushed into her chest, shattering bone to get into her intestines from above, and pulled the rope of guts out of her through the jagged shards of ribs. As she died, he let her fall to the ground, still gnawing on the entrails he had retrieved.

Pulling the gun from Aaron's belt, ignoring his gurgled pleas, she turned the pistol on Ferdinand, one of her oldest and dearest friends, and fired into the body.

Ferdinand, what was left of him, turned in surprise and whimpered

"Eesaah."

When she fired again, he roared and charged.

Lisa pulled the trigger again and again, praying with all her might to gods she had long abandoned in favor of science. The gun barked in her hand, kicking and throwing off her aim, but she continued to fire wildly. Ferdinand slowed, collapsing to his knees, red pulsing blood pulling at his knees as he watched her through bloodshot and rolling eyes. His jaw worked in sections as he tried to form words. Would he confess his love, apologize, or merely roar about his hunger?

Lisa shook her head. She couldn't. She steadied her shaking hand and raised the pistol to fire one more time. Even her novice experience couldn't miss at this range, and the back of Ferdinand's head exploded in a shower of gore.

Lisa choked back a sob as she dropped the gun and rose unsteadily to her feet. She realized the gunfire had stopped, but the discordant screams had not.

Turning towards the edge of the base, she saw swarms of the afflicted emerging from a red mist, the soldiers guarding the base nowhere to be seen. Just behind the waves of afflicted, coming closer one city block step at a time, was the salamander god Abhorrent.

Lisa set her mouth in a firm line. She had faced down challenges time and time again. From the slums of India, she had risen to become a prominent scientist. She had survived the mad flight across Texas. And now ... To have made it this far, to come so close to be moments away from safety and now to find herself here. She raised the gun, aimed at the massive giant bearing down on her, but she knew it would have no effect. She would be torn apart by the afflicted. Instead, she pressed the barrel against the bottom of her chin and pulled the trigger.

Click

Lisa screamed in rage and fear and frustration, every emotion bubbling out of her as she threw the gun away. She screamed again, breathing in the thick red mist that curled around her feet. She continued to scream even as she felt the bones in her legs shifting and pushing through her skin in jagged spikes. She screamed at the absurdity of it, she screamed at the pain, but mostly, she screamed in hunger.

John Baltisberger

John Baltisberger

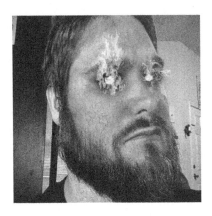

John Baltisberger is an author of speculative and genre fiction that often focuses on Jewish Elements. Through his writing, he has explored themes of mysticism, faith, sin, and personal responsibility. He lives in Austin, TX with his wife and his daughter.

Though mostly known for his bizarre blend of Jewish mysticism and splatter, John defies being labeled under any one genre. His work has spanned extreme horror, urban fantasy, science fiction, cosmic horror, epic verse, and he has even written a guide for mindful meditation. You can see his work and more at www.KaijuPoet.com

Also Available from St Rooster Books

From Tim Murr;

The Gray Man
978-1799252177
Lose This Skin; Collectected Short Works 1994-2011
978-1530351633
Conspiracy of Birds/Hounds of Doom
978-1516920631
City Long Suffering
978-1519588074
Motel on Fire; Stories
978-1543039016
Neon Sabbath; Stories
978-1721039708
My Skull is Full of Black Smoke; Stories
979-8680276099

Collection/Various Authors

To Be One With You; An Anthology of Parasitic Horror
2018 featuring Paul Kane, Marie O'Regan, Jeffery X
Martin, Peter Oliver Wonder, Adam Millard, DJ Tyrer,
David W Barbee, Ross Peterson
978-1724516787

Kids of the Black Hole; A Punksploitation Anthology
featuring Sarah Miner, Chris Hallock, Paul
Lubaczewski, and Jeremy Lowe
978-1072962724

*The Blind Dead Ride Out of Hell; A Literary Tribute to
the Amando de Ossorio Films* featuring Sam Richard,
Heather Drain, Paul Lubaczewski, Mark Zirbel,
Jeremy Lowe, and Jerome Reuter
979-8692365187

A New Life by Paul Lubaczewski
979-8615384066

Blood & Mud by John Baltisberger
979-8647568397

Made in United States
North Haven, CT
19 November 2021

11277939R00075